FAMILY TREE

FAMILY TREE

A collection of favourite poems and stories about all kinds of families

CHOSEN BY KAYE WEBB

HAMISH HAMILTON · LONDON

I am especially grateful to Denise Pearce, Felicity Trotman
and Ruth Marshall for their help and suggestions

HAMISH HAMILTON LTD
Published by the Penguin Group
27 Wrights Lane, London, London W8 5TZ, England
Penguin Books USA Inc., 375 Hudson Street, New York, New York 10014, USA
Penguin Books Australia Ltd, Ringwood, Victoria, Australia
Penguin Books Canada Ltd, 10 Alcorn Avenue, Toronto, Ontario, Canada M4V 3B2
Penguin Books (NZ) Ltd, 182–190 Wairau Road, Auckland 10, New Zealand

Penguin Books Ltd, Registered Offices: Harmondsworth, Middlesex, England

First published in Great Britain 1994 by Hamish Hamilton Ltd

A CIP catalogue record for this book is available from the British Library

ISBN 0–241–13161–8

Typeset by Datix International Limited, Bungay, Suffolk
Printed in England by Clays Ltd, St Ives plc

For Kate, John and Danny (my special family)

Contents

BROTHERS AND SISTERS

GRANDPARENTS

AUNTS, UNCLES AND SOME DISAGREEABLE COUSINS

FAMILIES CAN
BE DIFFERENT

When we are young and our lives are centred round the people we meet in our homes and schools, we are almost sure to think that everyone else has the same sort of family; the same kinds of aunts, uncles, cousins and grandparents, and, most especially, we expect other people's parents will say and do the same sort of things as ours.

Of course we'll notice that our friends have different birthday parties or holidays, but we don't really imagine their lives are very dissimilar from ours. I can remember how surprised I was to find out that a girl at school had a father who was so strict he made her learn a page of the dictionary every day, and recently, as a grown-up editor, I had a letter from one of my readers which said: 'Can you tell me if there are any books with quarrels in them, because my family always seems to be quarrelling, but no one else's does.'

That's why I decided to make this book, just to show you something about the different ways people behave in other kinds of families. And that's why I started with a quarrel!

Kaye Webb.

JULIANA HORATIA EWING

The Hatchet

FROM A Very Ill-Tempered Family

There are a lot of family quarrels in this book, but this is by far the most alarming (told by Isobel, the eldest sister).

*   *   *

We are a very ill-tempered family.

There are five of us; Philip and I are the eldest; we are twins. My name is Isobel.

'The children' are the other three. They are a good deal younger than Philip and I, so we have always kept them in order. I do not mean that we taught them to behave wonderfully well, but I mean that we made them give way to us older ones. Among themselves they squabbled dreadfully.

I very nearly killed Philip once. It makes me shudder to think of it, and I often wonder I ever could lose my temper again.

We were eight years old, and out in the garden together. We had settled to build a moss-house for my dolls, and had borrowed the hatchet out of the wood-house, without leave, to chop the stakes with. It was entirely my idea, and I had collected all the moss and most of the sticks. It was I, too, who had taken the hatchet. Philip had been very tiresome about not helping me in the hard part; but when I had driven in the sticks by leaning on them with all my weight, and had put in

13

bits of brushwood where the moss fell out and Philip laughed at me, and, in short, when the moss-house was beginning to look quite real, Philip was very anxious to work at it, and wanted the hatchet.

'You wouldn't help me over the hard work,' said I, 'so I shan't give it you now; I'll make my moss-house myself.'

'No, you won't,' said Philip.

'Yes, I shall,' said I.

'No, you won't,' he reiterated; 'for I shall pull it down as fast as you build it.'

'You'd better not,' I threatened.

Just then we were called in to dinner. I hid the hatchet, and Philip said no more; but he got out before me, and when I returned to work I found that the moss-house walls, which had cost me so much labour, were pulled to pieces and scattered about the shrubbery. Philip was not to be seen.

My heart had been so set upon my project that at first I could only feel the overwhelming disappointment. I was not a child who often cried, but I burst into tears.

I was sobbing my hardest when Philip sprang upon me in triumph, and laughing at my distress.

'I kept my promise,' said he, tossing his head, 'and I'll go on doing it.'

I am sure those shocks of fury which seize one like a fit must be a devil possessing one. In an instant my eyes were as dry as the desert in a hot wind, and my head reeling with passion. I ran to the hatchet, and came back brandishing it.

'If you touch one stake or bit of moss of mine again,' said I, 'I'll throw my hatchet at your head. I can keep promises too.'

My intention was only to frighten him. I relied on his not daring to brave such a threat; unhappily he relied on my not daring to carry it out. He took up some of my moss and threw it at me by way of reply.

I flung the hatchet!——

My Aunt Isobel has a splendid figure, with such grace and power as one might expect from her strong health and ready mind. I had not seen her at the moment, for I was blind with passion, nor had Philip, for his back was turned towards her. I did not see distinctly how she watched, as one watches for a ball, and caught the hatchet within a yard of Philip's head.

My Aunt Isobel has a temper much like the temper of the rest of the family. When she had caught it in her left hand she turned round and boxed my ears with her right hand till I could see less than ever. (I believe she suffered for that outburst for months afterwards. She was afraid she had damaged my hearing, as that sense is too often damaged or destroyed by the blows of ill-tempered parents, teachers, and nurses.)

Then she turned back and shook Philip as vigorously as she had boxed me. 'I saw you, you spiteful, malicious boy!' said my Aunt Isobel.

All the time she was shaking him, Philip was looking at her feet. Something that he saw absorbed his attention so fully that he forgot to cry.

'You're bleeding, Aunt Isobel,' said he, when she gave him breath enough to speak.

The truth was this: the nervous force which Aunt Isobel had summoned up to catch the hatchet seemed to cease when it was caught; her arm fell powerless, and the hatchet cut her ankle. That left arm was useless for many months afterwards, to my abiding reproach.

Philip was not hurt, but he might have been killed. Everybody told me so often that it was a warning to me to correct my terrible temper, that I might have revolted against the reiteration if the facts had been less grave. But I never can feel lightly about that hatchet-quarrel. It opened a gulf of possible wickedness and life-long misery, over the brink of which my temper would have dragged me, but for Aunt Isobel's strong arm and keen eye, and over which it might succeed in dragging me any day, unless I could cure myself of my besetting sin.

I never denied it. It was a warning.

HELEN CRESSWELL

FROM Absolute Zero

The next story is more about squabbles than real
quarrels, but the Bagthorpes have plenty of those.
There are five books about the Bagthorpe family, and
the situations they get into, but this seems to be the
funniest and the silliest. Mrs Fosdyke is their housekeeper . . .

*   *   *

Mrs Fosdyke, whom everyone had been ignoring, suddenly
let out a wild shriek. The row stopped dead. A lot of
shrieking went on in the Bagthorpe house, but to date
none of it had come from Mrs Fosdyke.

They all turned. She was standing in the doorway of the
pantry looking pale and distraught. In each hand she held
out a tin without a label.

'There's thousands of them!' she shrieked. 'And tops off
packets and holes in the sides of things!'

Only Mr Bagthorpe among those present had the faintest
idea what she was talking about. He wished himself at the
ends of the earth, the saltmines.

Mrs Fosdyke let the tins fall and watched them dully as
they rolled away over the tiles. She turned back, picked up
two more tins and let them go the same way. Jack thought
it obvious that she had gone mad, like Ophelia, but instead

of strewing flowers was rolling tins. They all stood there and watched till the tins finally came to rest. There was a silence. The next words clearly had to be spoken by Mrs Fosdyke, and they waited patiently. She started off by shaking her head. She shook her head for quite a long time and then at last spoke, but not really to them, more to herself.

'Plums and haricots, beans and tomatoes,' she intoned. She repeated it, as if it were a line of poetry.

'Plums and haricots, beans and tomatoes.'

Still no one else spoke. There seemed no answer to this kind of remark. After another pause she elaborated on her theme.

'Pineapple and mince, a dozen of cling peaches there was. Which is what, and whatever else?'

Mrs Fosdyke really did sound poetic as never before. She sounded like the Fool in *Lear*, rather. She turned back into the pantry and lifted two large packets and held them out. They were SUGAR COATED PUFFBALLS. The tops of both had been torn off. Again she wagged her head.

'Who?' she asked, half to herself. 'Who would ever? And why? What have I done? What can it mean?'

She paused after asking these five questions, and seemed to be casting around herself for an answer.

'Aha!' Jack heard Uncle Parker exclaim softly. 'I think I see the light.'

'I should've stopped at home,' mourned Mrs Fosdyke. 'I nearly never came. Not after last night.'

'What was wrong with last night?' demanded Grandma instantly. She had not been very interested in the tin rolling and poetry, particularly as it had interrupted a good argument. 'I enjoyed last night.'

'I've never been in trouble with the police,' went on Mrs Fosdyke. 'Never. And now this. I can't carry on.'

'Nonsense!' Grandma told her briskly. 'Jack, pick up those tins. Why are you rolling tins, Mrs Fosdyke?'

'Beans, peaches, tomatoes, plums. All sorts.'

'Somebody,' observed Uncle Parker, 'is going in for Competitions. Somebody, Mrs F., has been removing labels and lids from your pantry to send off with Competitions.'

'Not me,' said Jack promptly. He surfaced, holding the tins, caught sight of his father's face, and saw the truth written on it.

'The whole family's going in for Competitions,' blustered Mr Bagthorpe. He didn't care who found out about this so long as Uncle Parker never did. 'It's you that started it with that wretched Caribbean thing.' He had evidently decided that attack might be the best form of defence. Another row would act as a smokescreen.

'Which brand of cling peaches is it, I wonder,' mused Uncle Parker, 'that could be offering a month in the saltmines?'

'Luckily, my salt's all right,' soliloquized Mrs Fosdyke dismally, off on her own again. 'And my sugar. And my marmalades and jams is all right I suppose even without labels. It's my tins. You can't see through tins.'

This was incontestable. As they stood and pondered the matter Mrs Bagthorpe came in and pieced the story together and went into the pantry to inspect the damage.

'*Everyone* will have SUGAR COATED PUFFBALLS at breakfast now,' she announced, 'until they are all used up. We must eat them before they go soft. Some of us could have them for supper as well. When we find out who is responsible for this irresponsible act, then that person will probably be required to eat SUGAR COATED PUFFBALLS at every meal. It would have a certain poetic justice.'

'But the tins!' wailed Mrs Fosdyke. 'What about my tins?'

What happened about the tins was to affect the Bagthorpes' lives, and particularly their eating habits, for a long time to come. Meals could no longer be counted on in the way they once could. The family had never before, for instance, eaten processed peas with custard. Nor did they now, for that matter. But Mrs Bagthorpe had ruled that whatever tin was opened, its contents must be consumed, so they ate the peas first, then the custard separately afterwards. This particular combination came up quite often, because the sound of a tin of processed peas when shaken was practically indistinguishable from that of raspberries or prunes or fruit salad.

All the Bagthorpes took up Tin Shaking, and there would be fearful rows at first. William maintained that the tins could be identified by an elimination method, as in the game Master Mind, but his identification record was as bad as anyone else's. He was particularly bad at distinguishing between condensed soup and rice pudding, and the family often found themselves ending a meal with soup having started it in the same way. Sometimes they even got the same flavour. They were really furious with William when this happened.

In the end it was decided that a rota should be drawn up, and each Bagthorpe in turn should Shake a Tin, and try to produce the commodity Mrs Fosdyke required. Being Bagthorpes, they could not, of course, leave it at this, and developed a scoring system which was pinned on the pantry door next to the rota. Points were awarded from One to Five, depending on the accuracy of the guess.

You could only score Five by being dead accurate – in the case of soup, say, you actually had to produce the required flavour. Nobody got Five very often. Four was awarded to a near miss, such as raspberries for strawberries, and Three to successfully producing the right category, i.e. fruit as opposed to soup or savoury. Two was for a tin of tomatoes (Mrs Fosdyke had been hoarding them for months and one's chance of picking them out was at least five to one) and One point went to asparagus, which the Bagthorpes adored, and did not mind eating even at breakfast, following the mandatory SUGAR COATED PUFFBALLS.

For anything not in any of these five categories you simply scored nothing, with the sole exception that if you opened processed peas at breakfast you got five deducted. William actually went to the lengths of buying a tin of peas from the village shop, so that he could compare how it sounded when shaken, but this created violent opposition and was ruled out of order.

Grandpa was put in the rota at his own request. He had

great confidence in his new hearing aid (he had lost the old one in Grandma's Birthday Party Fire) and it must have been fairly effective because his scoring was more or less on a par with everyone else's.

The Bagthorpes, if they were in a good mood, quite enjoyed the Tin Shaking, but Mrs Fosdyke never did. She nearly gave in her notice over it.

'It's not good enough,' she told her cronies in the Fiddler's Arms, 'when I've done a beautiful sponge for a trifle, and one of them goes and opens a Condensed Oxtail. You could weep. And the best of it, for a grown man to have done it. If it'd been that Daisy, I could've understood it. He's mad, no doubt about it. Really mad.

PHILIPPA PEARCE

FROM What the Neighbours Did

In the middle of the night a fly woke Charlie, and
although he managed to hit it, it disappeared. But
Charlie still felt a tickling in his ear . . .

Charlie's family seems to be the sort we'd all like to
belong to!

*   *   *

The tickling in Charlie's ear continued. He could just
imagine the fly struggling in some passageway too narrow
for its wing-span. He longed to put his finger into his ear
and rattle it round, like a stick in a rabbit-hole; but he was
afraid of driving the fly deeper into his ear.

Wilson slept on.

Charlie stood in the middle of the bedroom floor, quivering and trying to think. He needed to see down his ear, or to get someone else to see down it. Wilson wouldn't do; perhaps Margaret would.

Margaret's room was next door. Charlie turned on the light as he entered: Margaret's bed was empty. He was startled, and then thought that she must have gone to the lavatory. But there was no light from there. He listened carefully: there was no sound from anywhere, except for the usual snuffling moans from the hall, where Floss slept and dreamt of dog-biscuits. The empty bed was mystifying; but Charlie had his ear to worry about. It sounded as if there were a pigeon inside it now.

Wilson asleep; Margaret vanished; that left Alison. But Alison was bossy, just because she was the eldest; and, anyway, she would probably only wake Mum. He might as well wake Mum himself.

Down the passage and through the door always left ajar. 'Mum,' he said. She woke, or at least half-woke, at once: 'Who is it? Who? Who? What's the matter? What? –'

'I've a fly in my ear.'

'You can't have.'

'It flew in.'

She switched on the bedside light, and, as she did so, Dad plunged beneath the bedclothes with an exclamation and lay still again.

Charlie knelt at his mother's side of the bed and she looked into his ear. 'There's nothing.'

'Something crackles.'

'It's wax in your ear.'

'It tickles.'

'There's no fly there. Go back to bed and stop imagining things.'

His father's arm came up from below the bedclothes. The hand waved about, settled on the bedside light and clicked it out. There was an upheaval of bedclothes and a comfortable grunt.

'Good night,' said Mum from the darkness. She was already allowing herself to sink back into sleep again.

'Good night,' Charlie said sadly. Then an idea occurred to him. He repeated his good night loudly and added some coughing, to cover the fact that he was closing the bedroom door behind him – the door that Mum kept open so that she could listen for her children. They had outgrown all that kind of attention, except possibly for Wilson. Charlie had shut the door against Mum's hearing because he intended to slip downstairs for a drink of water – well, for a drink and perhaps a snack. That fly-business had woken him up and also weakened him: he needed something.

He crept downstairs, trusting to Floss's good sense not to make a row. He turned the foot of the staircase towards the kitchen, and there had not been the faintest whimper from her, far less a bark. He was passing the dog-basket when he had the most unnerving sensation of something being wrong there – something unusual, at least. He could not have said whether he had heard something or smelt something – he could certainly have seen nothing in the blackness: perhaps some extra sense warned him.

'Floss?' he whispered, and there was the usual little scrabble and snuffle. He held out his fingers low down for Floss to lick. As she did not do so at once, he moved them towards her, met some obstruction –

'Don't poke your fingers in my eyes!' a voice said, very low-toned and cross. Charlie's first, confused thought was that Floss had spoken: the voice was familiar – but then a voice from Floss should *not* be familiar; it should be strangely new to him –

He took an uncertain little step towards the voice, tripped over the obstruction, which was quite wrong in shape and size to be Floss, and sat down. Two things now happened. Floss, apparently having climbed over the obstruction, reached his lap and began to lick his face. At the same time a human hand fumbled over his face, among the slappings of Floss's tongue, and settled over his mouth. 'Don't make a row! Keep quiet!' said the same voice. Charlie's mind cleared: he knew, although without under-standing, that he was sitting on the floor in the dark with Floss on his knee and Margaret beside him.

Her hand came off his mouth.

'What are you doing here, anyway, Charlie?'

'I like that! What about you? There was a fly in my ear.'

'Go on!'

'There was.'

'Why does that make you come downstairs?'

'I wanted a drink of water.'

'There's water in the bathroom.'

'Well, I'm a bit hungry.'

'If Mum catches you . . .'

'Look here,' Charlie said, 'you tell me what you're doing down here.'

Margaret sighed. 'Just sitting with Floss.'

'You can't come down and just sit with Floss in the middle of the night.'

'Yes, I can. I keep her company. Only at weekends, of course. No one seemed to realize what it was like for her when those puppies went. She just couldn't get to sleep for loneliness.'

'But the last puppy went weeks ago. You haven't been keeping Floss company every Saturday night since then.'

'Why not?'

Charlie gave up. 'I'm going to get my food and drink,'

he said. He went into the kitchen, followed by Margaret, followed by Floss.

They all had a quick drink of water. Then Charlie and Margaret looked into the larder: the remains of a joint; a very large quantity of mashed potato; most of a loaf; eggs; butter; cheese . . .

'I suppose it'll have to be just bread and butter and a bit of cheese,' said Charlie. 'Else Mum might notice.'

The National Union of Children

NUC has just passed a weighty resolution:
'Unless all parents raise our rate of pay
This action will be taken by our members
(The resolution comes in force today):
'Noses will not be blown (sniffs are in order),
Bedtime will get preposterously late,
Ice-cream and crisps will be consumed for breakfast,
Unwanted cabbage left upon the plate,

'Earholes and finger-nails can't be inspected,
Overtime (known as homework) won't be worked,
Reports from school will all say "Could do better",
Putting bricks back in boxes may be shirked.'

Roy Fuller

The National Association of Parents

Of course, NAP's answer quickly was forthcoming
(It was a matter of emergency),
It issued to the Press the following statement
(Its Secretary appeared upon TV):

'True that the so-called Saturday allowance
Hasn't kept pace with prices in the shops,
But neither have, alas, parental wages;
NUC's claim would ruin kind, hard-working pops.

'Therefore, unless that claim is now abandoned,
Strike action for us, too, is what remains;
In planning for the which we are in process
Of issuing, to all our members, canes.'

Roy Fuller

GERALD DURRELL

FROM Birds, Beasts and Relatives

Not many people will have had the chance to grow up on such an exciting island as Corfu, or have such an unusual family, but I think you will enjoy sharing this account of Gerald Durrell's wonderful birthday. He is ten, and Margo his sister and his brothers Larry and Leslie are practically grown up.

*   *   *

The day before my birthday, everybody started acting in a slightly more eccentric manner than usual. Larry, for some reason best known to himself, went about the house shouting 'Tantivy!' and 'Tally-ho' and similar hunting slogans. As he was fairly frequently afflicted in this way, I did not take much notice.

Margo kept dodging about the house carrying mysterious bundles under her arm and at one point I came face to face with her in the hall and noted, with astonishment, that her arms were full of multi-coloured decorations left over from Christmas. On seeing me, she uttered a squeak of dismay and rushed into her bedroom in such a guilty and furtive manner that I was left staring after her with open mouth.

Even Leslie and Spiro were afflicted, it seemed, and they kept going into mysterious huddles in the garden. From the snippets of their conversation that I heard, I could not make head or tail of what they were planning.

'In the backs seats,' Spiro said, scowling. 'Honest to Gods, Masters Leslies, I have dones it befores.'

'Well, if you're sure, Spiro,' Leslie replied doubtfully, 'but we don't want any broken legs or anything.'

Then Leslie saw me undisguisedly eavesdropping and asked me truculently what the hell I thought I was doing, eavesdropping on people's private conversations? Why didn't I go down to the nearest cliff and jump off? Feeling that the family were in no mood to be amicable, I took Roger off into the olive groves and for the rest of the day we ineffectually chased green lizards.

That night I had just turned down the lamp and snuggled into bed when I heard sounds of raucous singing, accompanied by gales of laughter coming through the olive groves. As the uproar got closer, I could recognize Leslie's and Larry's voices combined with Spiro's, each of them appearing to be singing a different song. It seemed as though they had been somewhere and celebrated too well. From the indignant whispering and shuffling going on in the corridor, I could tell that Margo and Mother had reached the same conclusion.

They burst into the villa, laughing hysterically at some witticism that Larry had produced and were shushed fiercely by Margo and Mother.

'Do be quiet,' said Mother. 'You'll wake Gerry. What have you been drinking?'

'Wine,' said Larry in a dignified tone. Then he hiccuped.

'Wine,' said Leslie. 'And then we danced and Spiro danced, and I danced, and Larry danced. And Spiro danced and then Larry danced and then I danced.'

'I think you had better go to bed,' said Mother.

'And then Spiro danced again,' said Leslie, 'and then Larry danced.'

'All right, dear, all right,' said Mother. 'Go to *bed* for

31

heaven's sake. Really, Spiro, I do feel that you shouldn't have let them drink so much.'

'Spiro danced,' said Leslie, driving the point home.

'I'll take him to bed,' said Larry. 'I'm the only sober member of the party.'

There was the sound of lurching feet on the tiles as Leslie and Larry, clasped in each other's arms, staggered down the corridor.

'I'm now dancing with *you*,' came Leslie's voice as Larry dragged him into his bedroom and put him to bed.

'I am sorrys, Mrs Durrells,' said Spiro, his deep voice thickened with wine, 'but I couldn't stops thems.'

'Did you get it?' said Margo.

'Yes, Missy Margos. Don'ts you worrys,' said Spiro. 'It's down with Costas.'

Eventually Spiro left and I heard Mother and Margo going to bed. It made a fittingly mysterious end to what had been a highly confusing day. But I soon forgot about the family's behaviour, as, lying in the dark wondering what my presents were going to be, I drifted off to sleep.

The following morning I woke and lay for a moment wondering what was so special about that day. Then I remembered. It was my birthday. I lay there savouring the feeling of having a whole day to myself when people would give me presents and the family would be forced to accede to any reasonable requests. I was just about to get out of bed and go and see what my presents were, when a curious uproar broke out in the hall.

'Hold its head. Hold its *head*,' came Leslie's voice.

'Look out, you're spoiling the decorations,' wailed Margo.

'Damn the bloody decorations,' said Leslie. 'Hold its *head*.'

'Now, now, dears,' said Mother. 'Don't quarrel.'

'Dear God,' said Larry in disgust, 'dung all over the floor.'

The whole of this mysterious conversation was accompanied by a strange pitta-pattering noise, as though someone were bouncing ping-pong balls on the tile floor of the hall. What on earth, I wondered, were the family up to now? Normally, at this time they were still lying, semi-conscious, groping bleary-eyed for their early morning cups of tea. I sat up in bed, preparatory to going into the hall to join in whatever fun was afoot, when my bedroom door burst open and a donkey, clad in festoons of coloured crêpe paper, Christmas decorations and with three enormous feathers attached skilfully between its large ears, came galloping into the bedroom, Leslie hanging grimly on to its tail shouting 'Woa, you bastard!'

'Language, dear,' said Mother, looking flustered in the doorway.

'You're spoiling the decorations,' screamed Margo.

'The sooner that animal gets out of here,' said Larry, 'the better. There's dung all over the hall now.'

'You frightened it,' said Margo.

'I didn't do anything,' said Larry indignantly. 'I just gave it a little push.'

The donkey skidded to a halt by my bedside and gazed at me out of enormous brown eyes. It seemed rather surprised. It shook itself vigorously so that the feathers between its ears fell off and then, very dexterously, hacked Leslie on the shin with its hind leg.

'Jesus!' roared Leslie, hopping around on one leg. 'It's broken my bloody leg.'

'Leslie, dear, there is no need to swear so much,' said Mother. 'Remember Gerry.'

'The sooner you get it out of that bedroom the better,' said Larry, 'otherwise the whole place will smell like a midden.'

'You've simply ruined its decorations,' said Margo, 'and it took me hours to put them on.'

But I was taking no notice of the family. The donkey had approached the edge of my bed, stared at me inquisitively for a moment and had then given a little throaty chuckle and thrust in my outstreched hands a grey muzzle as soft as everything soft I could think of – silkworm cocoons, newly-born puppies, sea pebbles, or the velvety feel of a tree frog. Leslie had now removed his trousers and was examining the bruise on his shin, cursing fluently.

'Do you like it, dear?' asked Mother.

Like it! I was speechless.

The donkey was a rich dark brown, almost a plum colour, with enormous ears like arum lilies, white socks over tiny polished hoofs as neat as a tap dancer's shoes. Running along her back was the broad black cross that denotes so proudly that her race carried Christ into Jerusalem (and has continued to be one of the most maligned domestic animals ever since) and round each great shining eye she had a neat white circle which denoted that she came from the village of Gastouri.

'You remember Katerina's donkey that you liked so much?' said Margo. 'Well, this is her baby.'

This, of course, made the donkey even more special. The donkey stood there looking like a refugee from a circus, chewing a piece of tinsel meditatively, while I scrambled out of bed and flung on my clothes. Where, I enquired breathlessly of Mother, was I to keep her? Obviously I couldn't keep her in the villa in view of the fact that Larry had just pointed out to Mother that she could, if she so wished, grow a good crop of potatoes in the hall.

'That's what the house Costas built is for,' said Mother.

I was beside myself with delight. What a noble, kindly, benevolent family I had! How cunningly they had kept the secret from me! How hard they had worked to deck the donkey out in its finery! Slowly and gently, as though she was some fragile piece of china, I led my steed out through the garden and round into the olive grove, opened the door of the little bamboo hut and took her inside. I thought I ought to try her for size, because Costas was a notoriously bad workman. The little house was splendid. Just big enough for her. I took her out again and tethered her to an olive tree on a long length of rope, then stayed for half an hour in a dream-like trance admiring her from every angle while she grazed placidly. Eventually I heard Mother calling me in to breakfast and I sighed with satisfaction. I had decided that, without any doubt whatsoever, and without wishing in any way to be partisan, this donkey was the finest donkey in the whole of the island of Corfu. For no reason that I could think of, I decided to call her Sally. I gave her a quick kiss on her silken muzzle and then went in to breakfast.

ETHEL TURNER

FROM Seven Little Australians

Now for two miserable families! In *Seven Little Australians* Judy is being sent away to boarding school because her father says she leads the other children into mischief.

* * *

There was a trunk standing in the hall, and a large, much-travelled portmanteau, and there were labels on them that said: 'Miss Helen Woolcot, The Misses Burton, Mount Victoria.'

In the nursery breakfast was proceeding spasmodically. Meg's blue eyes were all red and swollen with crying, and she was still sniffing audibly as she poured out the coffee. Pip had his hands in his pockets and stood on the hearthrug, looking gloomily at a certain plate, and refusing breakfast altogether; the General was crashing his own mug and plate joyously together; and Bunty was eating bread and butter in stolid silence.

Judy, white-faced and dry-eyed, was sitting at the table, and Nell and Baby were clinging to either arm. All the three days between that black Thursday and this doleful morning she had been obstinately uncaring. Her spirits had never seemed higher, her eyes brighter, her tongue sharper, than during that interval of days; and she had pretended to everyone, and her father, that she especially

36

thought boarding school must be great fun, and that she should enjoy it immensely.

But this morning she had collapsed altogether. All the time before, her hot, childish heart had been telling her that her father could not really be so cruel, that he did not really mean to send her away among strangers, away from dear, muddled old Misrule and all her sisters and brothers; he was only saying it to frighten her, she kept saying to herself, and she would show him she was not a chicken-hearted baby.

But on Sunday night, when she saw a trunk carried downstairs and filled with her things and labelled with her name, a cold hand seemed to close about her heart. Still, she said to herself, he was doing all this to make it seem more real.

But now it was morning, and she could disbelieve it no longer. Esther had come to her bedside and kissed her sorrowfully, her beautiful face troubled and tender. She had begged as she had never done before for a remission of poor Judy's sentence, but the Captain was adamant. It was she and she only who was always ringleader in everything; the others would behave when she was not there to incite them to mischief and go she should. Besides, he said, it would be the making of her. It was an excellent school he had chosen for her; the ladies who kept it were kind, but very firm, and Judy was being ruined for want of a firm hand. Which, indeed, was in a measure true.

Judy sat bolt upright in bed at the sight of Esther's sorrowful face.

'It's no good, dear; there's no way out of it,' she said gently. 'But you'll go like a brave girl, won't you, Ju-Ju? You always were the sort to die game, as Pip says.'

Judy gulped down a great lump in her throat, and her poor little face grew white and drawn.

37

'It's all right, Essie. There, you go on down to breakfast,' she said, in a voice that only shook a little; 'and please leave me the General, Esther; I'll bring him down with me.'

Esther deposited her little fat son on the pillow, and with one loving backward glance went out of the door.

And Judy pulled the little lad down into her arms, and covered the bedclothes right over both their heads, and held him in a fierce, almost desperate clasp for a minute or two, and buried her face in his soft, dimpled neck, and kissed it till her lips ached.

He fought manfully against these troublesome proceedings, and at last objected, with an angry scream, to being suffocated. So she flung back the clothes and got out of bed, leaving him to burrow about among the pillows, and pull feathers out of a hole in one of them.

She dressed in a quick nervous fashion, did her hair with more care than usual, and then picked up the General and took him along the passage into the nursery. All the others were here, and, with Esther, were evidently discussing her. The three girls looked tearful and protesting; Pip had just been brought to book for speaking disrespectfully of his father, and was looking sullen; and Bunty, not knowing what else to do at such a crisis, had fallen to catching flies, and was viciously taking off their wings.

It was a wretched meal. The bell sounded for the downstairs breakfast, and Esther had to go. Everyone offered Judy everything on the table, and spoke gently and politely to her. She seemed to be apart from them, a person not to be lightly treated in the dignity of this great trouble. Her dress, too, was quite new – a neat blue serge fresh from the dressmaker's hands; her boots were blacked and bright, her stockings guiltless of ventilatory chasms. All this helped to make her a Judy quite different from the harum-scarum one of a few days back, who used to come to breakfast looking as if her clothes had been pitchforked upon her.

Baby addressed herself to her porridge for one minute, but the next her feelings overcame her, and, with a little wail, she rushed round the table to Judy, and hung on her arm sobbing. This destroyed the balance of the whole company. Nell got the other arm and swayed to and fro in an access of misery. Meg's tears rained down into her teacup; Pip dug his heel in the hearthrug, and wondered what was the matter with his eyes; and even Bunty's appetite for bread and butter diminished.

Judy sat there silent; she had pushed back her unused plate, and sat regarding it with an expression of utter despair on her young face. She looked like a miniature tragedy queen going to immediate execution.

Presently Bunty got off his chair, covered up his coffee with his saucer to keep the flies out, and solemnly left the room. In a minute he returned with a pickle bottle, containing an enormous green frog.

'You can have it to keep for your very own, Judy,' he said, in a tone of almost reckless sadness. 'It'll keep you amused, perhaps, at school.'

Self-sacrifice could go no further, for this frog was the darling of Bunty's heart.

This stimulated the others; everyone fetched some offering to lay at Judy's shrine for a keepsake. Meg brought a bracelet, plaited out of the hair of a defunct pet pony. Pip gave his three-bladed pocket-knife. Nell a pot of musk that she had watered and cherished for a year, Baby had a broken-nosed doll that was the Benjamin of her large family.

'Put them in the trunk, Meg – there's room on top, I think,' Judy said in a choking voice, and deeply touched by these gifts. 'Oh! and, Bunty, dear! put a cork over the f – f – frog, will you? it might get lost, poor thing! in that b – b – big box.'

'All right,' said Bunty. 'You'll take c – c – care of it, w – won't you, Judy? Oh dear, oh – h – h! – boo – hoo!'

Then Esther came in, still troubled-looking.

'The dogcart is round,' she said. 'Are you ready, Ju, dearest? Dear little Judy! be brave, little old woman.'

But Judy was white as death, and utterly limp. She suffered Esther to put her hat on, to help her into her new jacket, to put her gloves into her hand. She submitted to being kissed by the whole family, to be half carried downstairs by Esther, to be kissed again by the girls, then by the two good-natured domestics, who, in spite of her peccadilloes, had a warm place in their hearts for her.

Esther and Pip lifted her into the dogcart, and she sat in a little, huddled-up way, looking down at the group on the veranda with eyes that were absolutely tragic in their utter despair. Her father came out, buttoning his overcoat, and saw the look.

'What foolishness is this?' he said irascibly. 'Esther – great heavens! are you making a goose of yourself, too?' – there were great tears glistening in his wife's beautiful eyes. 'Upon my soul, one would think I was going to take the child to be hanged, or at least was going to leave her in a penitentiary.'

A great dry sob broke from Judy's white lips.

'If you'll let me stay, Father, I'll never do another thing to vex you; and you can thrash me instead, ever so hard.'

It was her last effort, her final hope, and she bit her poor quivering lip till it bled while she waited for his answer.

'Let her stay – oh! do let her stay, we'll be good always,' came in a chorus from the veranda. And, 'Let her stay, John, *please*!' Esther called, in a tone as entreating as any of the children.

But the Captain sprang into the dogcart and seized the reins from Pat in a burst of anger.

'I think you're all demented!' he cried. 'She's going to a thoroughly good home, I've paid a quarter in advance already, and I can assure you good people I'm not going to waste it.'

He gave the horse a smart touch with the whip, and in a minute the dogcart had flashed out of the gate, and the small, unhappy face was lost to sight.

BRIAN FAIRFAX LUCY AND
PHILIPPA PEARCE

FROM The Children of the House

Charlecote Park in Warwickshire really exists and now belongs to the National Trust, and the children you read about really did live there before the First World War. They had a very severe father and were always hungry, but they managed to enjoy themselves secretly.

*   *   *

They never met their parents until after breakfast, which was now brought to them by Elsie, the little between-maid. She was on their side. They would never forget that, when she had been very new in service at the Hall, she had carried a plum-cake up to them from the dining-room, under the impression that the children had the same food as their parents.

The gong sounded for prayers. Soberly the children went down the front stairs to the dining-room. They entered in order of age, Laura first, and in the same order kissed their parents and took their places. Walter Mark and Ernest, the footman, brought in two benches for the servants to sit on, and Walter handed Sir Robert his Bible and Prayer-book. No one ever spoke, and there was a particular silence as the rest of the household staff filed in – Lady Hatton's French maid, Hortense; Mrs Ashley, the cook; Alice, the head housemaid; Elsie, the between-maid;

the under-housemaid; and the kitchen-maid. Ernest shut the door after the last of them, and then he and Walter took their seats at the ends of the two rows.

Sir Robert read from the Bible. Then, at his 'Let us pray', everyone turned to kneel. This was the moment when Hugh and Margaret – Laura felt herself growing too old for it – sometimes tried to catch the eye of a friend from beyond the baize door, to force even a quarter-smile; but today neither was in the mood. They all sensed trouble brewing.

The servants had filed out again in the order of their entry; Ernest and Walter had removed the benches, and themselves.

'Shut the door, Laura,' said their father. 'I wish to speak to you all.'

Their hearts sank. Could their adventure already be known; or was this just an ordinary lecture?

'Now,' said Sir Robert, when Laura was back in her place. 'The holidays have started and tonight Tom comes home. I warn you that I will not tolerate any wildness, lateness for meals, untidiness, disobedience, or misbehaviour in any way. I know that Tom is often your ringleader, and if he does not mend his ways, I shall send him away with a tutor. I am also prepared, if necessary, to hire a tutor here so that you do lessons all through the holidays. Do you understand?'

'Yes, Papa.'

Lady Hatton spoke more gently. 'But, of course, we know you will all wish to start your holidays by being good.' They realized that they ought to feel guilty: it was so much too late to start the holidays by being good, since this morning.

'Hugh,' said his father, 'you will ride this morning.'

'Yes, Papa.'

'But as I shall be busy with papers, you will ride with William.' The clouds rolled back from Hugh's morning: ride with *William*!

Their mother took over now. 'This afternoon Papa and I have to attend a meeting. I want you all to take a rice pudding to old Mrs Higgs in the village. You can go in the pony-trap – Laura had better drive. After that, you may play in the garden.'

'Be careful not to spoil your clothes in any way,' said their father, 'as I certainly cannot afford to get you new ones.'

'Now all of you run along to the schoolroom and read your books. Be especially quiet, as Papa has several people to see in his study.'

'No running up and down the passage,' said Sir Robert.

'No, indeed,' said their mother.

They were dismissed; they were safe. Their adventure was undiscovered, after all. And this afternoon, after the expedition in the pony-trap, they could boil the moorhen's eggs. In fact, since their parents would be out, the whole afternoon was theirs. And in the evening Tom would come home.

NOEL STREATFEILD

from A Vicarage Family

The Vicarage Family were not all unhappy but they had a saintly father who didn't understand the problems of his growing daughters – one of whom (Victoria, in this extract) grew up to be the famous author of *Ballet Shoes*.

*   *   *

Lunch on Sundays was always the same: a roast joint, usually beef, in which case it was served with Yorkshire pudding, followed by apple tart and custard. Afterwards, because it was Sunday, the one sweet of the Lenten week was eaten, chosen by each in turn according to age, from one of the many boxes given to the family last Christmas. Chocolates, except on special occasions, were only eaten once a day, so sometimes the Christmas boxes lasted until midsummer. During Lent six chocolates were put away each week to be given to a blind child in the parish on Easter Day.

After lunch the envelope was opened. Inside was an invitation card, which said that Joyce was giving a party from four o'clock to eight o'clock and she hoped Isobel, Victoria and Louise would be able to come. There would be competitions and a conjurer. It was this last which drew excited murmurs from the girls.

There were many parties, especially round Christmas,

but they were usually only games and dancing; a conjurer was a rare treat at a time when for children such as the Strangeways there was no entertainment save an occasional magic lantern, except those they made themselves. Other children had things called phonographs on which a black tube spun round and tunes came out, such as *A Whistler and his Dog*, but not the Strangeways, such things not only cost too much but were looked at in dismay by their father, who had no love for any invention he had not known as a child in his own home. True, he accepted gas and was to accept electricity but all his life he sighed for lamps.

'Don't get too excited about the conjurer,' their mother warned. 'The party is on the Saturday before Holy Week so I doubt if Daddy will let you go.'

'It's going to be awkward for him saying "no" as Mr Sedman's a churchwarden,' Victoria suggested.

Her mother wanted to snap but refrained.

'I've yet to hear your father say "yes" to something he did not approve of.'

Louise looked anxious.

'I do hope he lets us go. It's been a very long Lent this year.'

On Sunday afternoon the children were taken by Miss Herbert to the children's service, so asking their father had to wait until after tea. They did not mind the children's service which was, though they did not know it, a model of what a service for children should be. There were plenty of popular hymns. A reading from the Bible. A short talk on a theme suitable for children, another hymn and then, what all the children waited for – a story. How the vicar managed to find a new, absorbing story Sunday after Sunday amazed the adults, but the truth was he was a splendid story-teller and could produce a first-class story without much material.

When years later Victoria wrote books for children and was asked whether her talent was inherited she always said 'yes', thinking back to those Sunday afternoons.

Sunday tea for the girls was in the schoolroom supervised by Miss Herbert. Because it was Sunday the fast was lifted and there was both jam and a home-made cake. Usually on the Sundays in Lent the girls lingered over tea, enjoying the food they would not taste again for a week, but today they were anxious to get downstairs to learn whether or not they would be allowed to go to Joyce's party.

In the drawing-room the children's mother had broken the news of the invitation to their father. He looked at her with a worried face.

'How awkward, and how peculiar of Sedman to give a party in Lent. In the ordinary way I would have told the children to refuse, but as we are leaving it seems unkind.'

The children's mother helped herself to a sandwich.

'I expect he would be hurt. He's going to miss you.'

'And I him, dear man; yes, I think perhaps the girls must go, but because I say yes this time they must not think it could happen again.'

The girls had not thought it could happen once! Before they came down Isobel had implored Victoria not to argue if the invitation had to be refused.

'It won't do any good and will only end in a row.'

'If Daddy says no I shall cry,' said Louise. 'I do so want to see the conjurer.'

Isobel looked at Victoria.

'That might be an idea, Daddy hates her to cry.'

Victoria stumped off to wash her hands, which had to be done before they went to the drawing-room.

'I'd much rather have a good argument, but if dear little Louise wants to cry, let her.'

So it came as an anticlimax when, as the girls came into

47

the drawing-room, Isobel holding the invitation, their father said:

'I have decided that as we are leaving the parish it would be unkind if you refused the party, so you may accept.'

The girls fell on him.

'Oh, thank you, Daddy,' said Isobel as she kissed him. Louise hung round his neck.

'Did you know there was going to be a conjurer?'

Victoria rubbed her cheek against his.

'I can't pretend I like Joyce much but I'm glad we can go to her party, it's her birthday so there's sure to be a terrific cake.'

That made her father think.

'But listen, darlings, although you may go it does not mean that you forget it is Lent. Just stick to bread and butter for tea and, of course, no dressing up.'

Horrified, the girls moved away from him. Eating only bread and butter at a party was bad, but no dressing up was much worse.

'But it's a *party*, Daddy.' Isobel held out the invitation. 'Look, a proper invitation card, everybody will wear party frocks.'

'You couldn't mean we're to wear our school skirts and jerseys,' said Victoria. 'If we do I'd rather not go.'

Louise's eyes were full of tears.

'I haven't worn my muslin with the pink sash since Christmas.'

Their father looked at their mother for help.

'Couldn't they wear what they've got on? They look very nice to me.'

The three girls gave a protesting howl.

'Daddy!'

'Nice!' said Louise. 'This smock is so old it's falling to pieces.'

Victoria stuck her chin in the air.

'If I have to go to a party in a frock where the sleeves are a different colour to the dress I'm not going.'

'Mummy, make Daddy see we can't go in our Sundays,' Isobel pleaded. 'Nobody, absolutely nobody, could say I look nice in this!'

Her mother looked and thought that perhaps Isobel was right.

'They could wear their velvets,' she suggested.

Victoria almost stamped her foot.

'But they're nearly as awful – at least mine and Louise's are.'

Their father felt sad. In his home there had never been scenes like this about clothes. Were his children thinking too much of worldly things? He quoted quietly: '"Consider the lilies of the field . . ."'

That maddened Victoria.

'Oh, Daddy! What's that got to do with us? Nobody could say that Solomon in all his glory was not arrayed better than us in our Sundays *or* our velvets.'

Their father did not mean to be unkind but he was a truly unworldly man and could not believe, provided they were suitably dressed, that it mattered what his daughters wore. And also he was convinced that they should have better things to think about than frocks. He got up.

'I must go to my study. Now Mummy and I don't want to hear any more about what you will wear at the party. You will accept the invitation, Isobel, and you will go in the frocks you have on now.'

Prayer for a Happy Family

God bless Mum and Dad and Baby
God bless me and sister Sue.
God bless Auntie Bloss, and maybe
Bless my Uncle Ernest too.
God bless Granma, God bless Grandy,
God bless cousins Dick and Dot.
God bless Marge and little Mandy,
Though you needn't bless a lot.
Bless my home and bless my teacher,
Stop her telling tales to Mum.
Bless Aunt Rose if you can reach her
Safe at rest in Kingdom Come.
Bless my family and guard them
Keep them safe and free-from-sin.
Now that's finished we'll discard them,
This is where my prayers begin:

PLEASE GOD DO LET AUNTIE BLOSS ASK
GRANMA TO TELL MUM TO MAKE DAD
SAY I REALLY CAN KEEP A RABBIT.

Ursula Moray Williams

MARGARET SIDNEY

FROM Five Little Peppers and How They Grew

I wonder if you will have noticed that all the really happy family stories are ones where they are so busy working away to get enough money to eat or pay the rent that they don't really have time or the energy for quarrels, and even very small pleasures give them such delight.

My particular favourite is *Five Little Peppers*. It was written over a hundred years ago. The children had no father and no money; but they had a wonderful mother and a remarkable sister called Polly, and also a dreadful old stove which was always going out. Once the whole family got the measles very badly, Polly worst of all, and her eyes were in danger. This story happens on the very day when the bandage is to be taken off, and the rest of the family have prepared a surprise for her. Here it comes:

*   *   *

The children all had to play 'clap in and clap out' in the bedroom while *it* came, and 'stagecoach', too – 'anything to make a noise,' Ben said. And then after they got nicely started in the game, he would be missing to help about the mysterious thing in the kitchen, which was safe, since Polly couldn't see him go on account of her bandage. So she didn't suspect in the least. And although the rest were

51

almost dying to be out in the kitchen, they conscientiously stuck to their bargain to keep Polly occupied. Only Joel *would* open the door and peep once, and then Phronsie behind him began, 'Oh, I see the sto –' but David swooped down on her in a twinkling and smothered the rest by tickling her.

Once they came very near having the whole thing pop out.

'Whatever is that noise in the kitchen?' asked Polly as they all stopped to take breath after the scuffle of 'stagecoach'. 'It sounds just like grating.'

'I'll go and see,' cried Joel promptly, and then he flew out where his mother and Ben and two men were at work on a big, black thing in the corner. The old stove, strange to say, was nowhere to be seen. Something else stood in its place – a shiny, black affair with a generous supply of oven doors and altogether such a comfortable, homelike look about it, as if it would say, 'I'm going to make sunshine in this house!'

'Oh, Joel,' cried his mother, turning around on him with very black hands. 'You *haven't* told!'

'No,' said Joel, 'but she's hearin' the noise, Polly is.'

'*Hush*!' said Ben to one of the men.

'We can't put it up without some noise,' the man replied, 'but we'll be as still as we can.'

'Isn't it a big one, ma?' asked Joel in the loudest of stage whispers that Polly on the other side of the door couldn't have failed to hear if Phronsie hadn't laughed just then.

'Go back, Joe, do,' said Ben. 'Play tag – *anything*,' he implored. 'We'll be through in a few minutes.'

'It takes forever!' said Joel, disappearing within the bedroom door. Luckily for the secret, Phronsie just then ran a pin sticking up on the arm of the old chair into her finger, and Polly, while comforting her, forgot to question

Joel. And then the mother came in, and though she had ill-concealed hilarity in her voice, she kept chattering and bustling around with Polly's supper to such an extent that there was no chance for a word to be got in.

Next morning it seemed as if the little brown house would turn inside out with joy.

'Oh, mammy!' cried Polly, jumping into her arms the first thing as Dr Fisher untied the bandage. 'My eyes are *new*! Just the same as if I'd just got 'em! Don't they *look* different?' she asked earnestly, running to the cracked glass to see for herself.

'No,' said Ben, 'I hope not; the same brown ones, Polly.'

'Well,' said Polly, hugging first one and then another, 'everybody looks different through them, anyway.'

'Oh,' cried Joel, 'come out into the kitchen, Polly. It's a great deal better out there.'

'May I?' asked Polly, who was in such a twitter looking at everything that she didn't know which way to turn.

'Yes,' said the doctor, smiling at her.

'Well, then,' sang Polly, 'come, mammy, we'll go first. Isn't it just lovely – oh, *mammy*!' And Polly turned so very pale and looked as if she were going to tumble right over that Mrs Pepper grasped her arm in dismay.

'*What is it?*' she asked, pointing to the corner, while all the children stood round in the greatest excitement.

'Why,' cried Phronsie, 'it's a *stove* – don't you know, Polly?'

But Polly gave one plunge across the room, and before anybody could think, she was down on her knees with her arms flung right around the big, black thing, and laughing and crying over it, all in the same breath!

And then they all took hold of hands and danced around it like wild little things, while Dr Fisher stole out silently, and Mrs Pepper laughed till she wiped her eyes to see them go.

'We aren't ever goin' to have any more burned bread,' sang Polly, all out of breath.

'Nor your back isn't goin' to break any more,' panted Ben with a very red face.

'Hooray!' screamed Joel and David, to fill any pause that might occur, while Phronsie gurgled and laughed at everything just as it came along. And then they all danced and capered again – all but Polly, who was down before the precious stove examining and exploring into ovens and everything that belonged to it.

'Oh, ma,' she announced, coming up to Mrs Pepper, who had been obliged to fly to her sewing again, and exhibiting a very crocky face and a pair of extremely smutty hands, 'it's most all ovens, and it's just splendid!'

'I know it,' answered her mother, delighted in the joy of her child. 'My! How black you are, Polly!'

'Oh, I wish,' cried Polly, as the thought struck her, 'that Dr Fisher could see it! Where did he go to, ma?'

'I guess Dr Fisher has seen it before,' said Mrs Pepper, and then she began to laugh. 'You haven't ever asked where the stove came from, Polly.'

And to be sure, Polly had been so overwhelmed that if the stove had really dropped from the clouds, it would have been small matter of astonishment to her, as long as it had *come*; that was the main thing!

'Mammy,' said Polly, turning around slowly with the stove lifter in her hand, 'did Dr Fisher bring that stove?'

'He didn't exactly *bring* it,' answered her mother, 'but I guess he knew something about it.'

'Oh, he's the splendidest, *goodest* man,' cried Polly, 'that ever breathed! Did he *really* get us that stove?'

'Yes,' said Mrs Pepper, 'he would. I couldn't stop him. I don't know how he found out you wanted one so bad; but he said it must be kept as a surprise when your eyes got well.'

'And he saved my eyes!' cried Polly, full of gratitude. 'I've got a stove and two new eyes, mammy. Just to think!'

'We ought to be good after all our mercies,' said Mrs Pepper thankfully, looking around on her little group. Joel was engaged in the pleasing occupation of seeing how far he could run his head into the biggest oven, and then pulling it out to exhibit its blackness, thus engrossing the others in a perfect hubbub.

'I'm going to bake my doctor some little cakes,' declared Polly when there was comparative quiet.

'Do, Polly,' cried Joel, 'and then leave one or two over.'

'No,' said Polly, 'we can't have any, because these must be very nice. Mammy, can't I have some white on top, just once?' she pleaded.

'I don't know,' dubiously replied Mrs Pepper. 'Eggs are dreadful dear, and –'

'I don't care,' said Polly recklessly. 'I must just once, for Dr Fisher.'

'I tell you, Polly,' said Mrs Pepper, 'what you might do – you might make him some little apple tarts; most everyone likes them, you know.'

'Well,' said Polly with a sigh, 'I s'pose they'll *have* to do; but *sometime*, mammy, I'm going to bake him a big cake, so there!'

EVE GARNETT

FROM The Family from One End Street

The neighbours pitied Mrs Ruggles for having such a large family, but Mr Ruggles was proud of the seven girls and boys all growing up fine and strong one behind the other like steps in a ladder, and however hard-up they were, they were always happy.

*   *   *

In spite of a wife and seven children (not to speak of Ideas) Mr Ruggles was a very contented sort of man. When the wind was in the East and blew bits of dirt from his dustbins and cart into his eyes and mouth he spat and swore a bit, but it was soon over. So long as he had his job and his family were well and happy, and he could smoke his pipe and work in his garden, see his mates at the Working Men's Club once or twice a week, dream about his Pig, and have a good Blow Out on Bank Holidays, he wanted nothing more. Mr Ruggles always 'went a bust' as he expressed it, on Bank Holidays. For the August one he would do any odd job he could get, and take the whole family for a day to the sea six miles away. They would start off about eight o'clock, by the first bus, each member of the family carrying something, one a Thermos, another a loaf or a bag of buns, and Mrs Ruggles bringing up the rear with the last baby in a folding push-pram. If it was fine they would have a great day! First a walk along the

promenade, then Dinner on the beach about twelve – all the Ruggles sitting in a row *gorging* pork-pies and doughnuts and bananas, while the sea-gulls flew expectantly round.

After dinner they would go on the Pier and put pennies in all the automatic machines, and watch games of Football, Cricket and Boxing, or thrillers like the 'Burning House', in which the firemen rescued a lady in her nightdress from the top bedroom, or, best of all, 'The Execution', a drama in three acts – 'The Condemned Cell', 'The Walk to the Scaffold', and 'The Hanging'. This last was so popular that Mr Ruggles often wasted as much as threepence on it, although Rosie said it was 'highly unsuitable' for children. After the Pier they usually paddled and Mrs Ruggles enjoyed this more than anyone.

'I has my hands in water every day,' she would say, 'and now I'm going to give my feet a turn!'

In the afternoon there were the Pierrots or the Band, or, if you were careful and knew your way about, and secured chairs in the right spot, both at once – Pierrots to the right, Band to the left – confusing at times, but none the less enjoyable, especially when you knew you were getting both free.

After this there was Tea. Tea was a great feature of the day, and the Ruggles would usually join with some of their friends and patronize one of the numerous shanties on the Front. There were dozens of these, and every kind of tea was advertised. 'High Tea', 'Devonshire Tea', 'Plain Tea', 'Fish Tea', or 'Fish *and* Chips tea', in fact, the choice was overwhelming! But the Ruggles were experienced! They looked carefully inside before entering, and if they saw a notice to the effect that 'tea and minerals will not be served to those bringing their own food', they moved on, for they always brought their own bread and butter and tea too sometimes, for these, though necessary, cost money, and they preferred to spend that on shrimps and cockles and other delicacies when at the seaside.

Most of the 'shanties' had names such as 'Home Sweet Home', 'The Nut-Shell', 'The Old Firm', or 'Where the Kettle Sings', but the Ruggles favourite bore the legend, 'Tea as Mother Makes it'. Here you were allowed your own bread and butter, and 'Mother', a lady of gigantic proportions, gave you, Mr Ruggles declared, more shrimps to the pint than any other establishment in the town.

Even a wet Bank Holiday was enjoyable at Brightwell, for the day could be spent under cover in the Amusement Arcade with sometimes a finish up at the Cinema.

E. NESBIT

The Jungle Game

FROM The Wouldbegoods

There are six Bastables: Dora, Dickie, Alice, Noel, H.O. and Oswald, who usually tells about their 'hopeful' deeds. This is the most disastrous they ever thought of.

*　　　*　　　*

Next morning when we were having breakfast and the two strangers were sitting there so pink and clean, Oswald suddenly said –

'I know; we'll have a jungle in the garden.'

And the others agreed, and we talked about it till brek was over. The little strangers only said 'I don't know' whenever we said anything to them.

After brekker Oswald beckoned his brothers and sisters mysteriously apart and said –

'Do you agree to let me be captain today, because I thought of it?'

And they said they would.

Then he said, 'We'll play *Jungle Book*, and I shall be Mowgli. The rest of you can be what you like – Mowgli's father and mother, or any of the beasts.'

'I don't suppose they know the book,' said Noel. 'They don't look as if they read anything, except at lesson times.'

'Then they can go on being beasts all the time,' Oswald said. 'Anyone can be a beast.'

So it was settled.

We all thought of different things. Of course first we dressed up pillows in the skins of beasts and set them about on the grass to look as natural as we could. And then we got Pincher, and rubbed him all over with powdered slate-pencil, to make him the right colour for Grey Brother. But he shook it all off, and it had taken an awful time to do. Then Alice said –

'Oh, I know!' and she ran off to Father's dressing-room, and came back with the tube of *crème d'amande pour la barbe et les mains*, and we squeezed it on Pincher and rubbed it in, and then the slate-pencil stuff stuck all right, and he rolled in the dust-bin of his own accord, which made him just the right colour. He is a very clever dog, but soon after he went off and we did not find him till quite late in the afternoon. Denny helped with Pincher, and with the wild-beast skins, and when Pincher was finished he said –

'Please, may I make some paper birds to put in the trees? I know how.'

And of course we said 'Yes', and he only had red ink and newspapers, and quickly he made quite a lot of large paper birds with red tails. They didn't look half bad on the edge of the shrubbery.

While he was doing this he suddenly said, or rather screamed, 'Oh?'

And we looked, and it was a creature with great horns and a fur rug – something like a bull and something like a minotaur – and I don't wonder Denny was frightened. It was Alice, and it was first-class.

Up to now all was not yet lost beyond recall. It was the stuffed fox that did the mischief – and I am sorry to own it was Oswald who thought of it. He is not ashamed of having *thought* of it. That was rather clever of him. But he knows now that it is better not to take other people's foxes

and things without asking, even if you live in the same
house with them.

It was Oswald who undid the back of the glass case in
the hall and got out the fox with the green and grey duck
in its mouth, and when the others saw how awfully like life
they looked on the lawn, they all rushed off to fetch the
other stuffed things. Uncle has a tremendous lot of stuffed
things. He shot most of them himself – but not the fox, of
course. There was another fox's mask, too, and we hung
that in a bush to look as if the fox was peeping out. And
the stuffed birds we fastened on to the trees with string.
The duck-bill – what's its name? – looked very well sitting
on his tail with the otter snarling at him. Then Dicky had

an idea; and though not nearly so much was said about it
afterwards as there was about the stuffed things, I think
myself it was just as bad, though it was a good idea, too.
He just got the hose and put the end over a branch of the
cedar-tree. Then we got the steps they clean windows with,
and let the hose rest on the top of the steps and run. It was
to be a waterfall, but it ran between the steps and was only
wet and messy; so we got Father's mackintosh and uncle's
and covered the steps with them, so that the water ran
down all right and was glorious, and it ran away in a
stream across the grass where we had dug a little channel
for it – and the otter and the duck-bill-thing were as if in
their native haunts. I hope all this is not very dull to read

about. I know it was jolly good fun to do. Taking one thing with another, I don't know that we ever had a better time while it lasted.

The lawn under the cedar was transformed into a dream of beauty, what with the stuffed creatures and the paper-tailed things and the waterfall. And Alice said –

'I wish the tigers did not look so flat.' For of course with pillows you can only pretend it is a sleeping tiger getting ready to make a spring out at you. It is difficult to prop up tiger-skins in a life-like manner when there are no bones inside them, only pillows and sofa cushions. 'What about the beer-stands?' I said. And we got two out of the cellar. With bolsters and string we fastened insides to the tigers – and they were really fine. The legs of the beer-stands did for tigers' legs. It was indeed the finishing touch.

And then a really sad event instantly occurred, which was not really our fault, and we did not mean to.

That Daisy girl had been mooning indoors all the afternoon with the *Jungle Books*, and now she came suddenly out, just as Dicky and Noel had got under the tigers and were shoving them along to fright each other. Of course, this is not in the Mowgli book at all: but they did look jolly like real tigers, and I am very far from wishing to blame the girl, though she little knew what would be the awful consequence of her rash act. But for her we might have got out of it all much better than we did.

What happened was truly horrid.

As soon as Daisy saw the tigers she stopped short, and uttering a shriek like a railway whistle she fell flat on the ground.

'Fear not, gentle Indian maid,' Oswald cried, thinking with surprise that perhaps after all she did know how to play, 'I myself will protect thee.' And he sprang forward with the native bow and arrows out of uncle's study.

The gentle Indian maiden did not move.

'Come hither,' Dora said, 'let us take refuge in yonder covert while this good knight does battle for us.'

Dora might have remembered that we were savages, but she did not. And that is Dora all over. And still the Daisy girl did not move.

Then we were truly frightened. Dora and Alice lifted her up, and her mouth was a horrid violet-colour and her eyes half shut. She looked horrid. Not at all like fair fainting damsels, who are always of an interesting pallor. She was green, like a cheap oyster on a stall.

We did what we could, a prey to alarm as we were. We rubbed her hands and let the hose play gently but persever-ingly on her unconscious brow. The girls loosened her dress, though it was only the kind that comes down straight without a waist. And we were all doing what we could as hard as we could, when we heard the click of the front gate. There was no mistake about it.

'I hope whoever it is will go straight to the front door,' said Alice. But whoever it was did not. There were feet on the gravel, and there was the uncle's voice, saying in his hearty manner –

'This way. This way. On such a day as this we shall find our young barbarians all at play somewhere about the grounds.'

And then, without further warning, the uncle, three other gentlemen and two ladies burst upon the scene.

We had no clothes on to speak of – I mean us boys. We were all wet through. Daisy was in a faint or a fit, or dead, none of us then knew which. And all the stuffed animals were there staring the uncle in the face. Most of them had got a sprinkling, and the otter and the duck-bill brute were simply soaked. And three of us were dark brown. Concealment, as so often happens, was impossible.

The quick brain of Oswald saw, in a flash, exactly how it would strike theuncle, and his brave younfg blood ran cold in his veins. His heart stood still.

'What's all this – eh, what?' said the tones of the wronged uncle.

Oswald spoke up and said it was jungles we were playing, and he didn't know what was up with Daisy. He explained as well as anyone could, but words were now in vain.

The uncle had a Malacca cane in his hand, and we were but ill prepared to meet the sudden attack. Oswald and H. O. caught it worst. The other boys were under the tigers – and of course my uncle would not strike a girl. Denny was a visitor and so got off. But it was bread and water for us for the next three days, and our own rooms. I will not tell you how we sought to vary the monotonousness of imprisonment. Oswald thought of taming a mouse, but he could not find one. The reason of the wretched captives might have given way but for the gutter that you can crawl along from our room to the girls'. But I will not dwell on this because you might try it yourselves, and it really is dangerous. When my father came home we got the talking to, and we said we were sorry – and we really were – especially about Daisy, though she had behaved with muffishness, and then it was settled that we were to go into the country and stay till we had grown into better children.

The Perfect Family

What could be happier and sweeter than the name of father, mother, and children (that is, a family) where the children hang on their parents' arms and exchange many kisses with them, and where husband and wife are so drawn to one another by love and choice, and experience such friendship between themselves that what one wants, the other also chooses, and what one says, the other maintains in silence as if he had said it himself; where all good and evil is held in common, the good all the happier, the adversity all the lighter, because shared by two.

Albrecht von Eyb, 15th century

MOTHERS

Mothers are the most difficult members of a family to describe, perhaps because their moods are often changing – sometimes patient and loving, sometimes irritable and cross about things which don't seem so important to their children, but usually turning up trumps on important occasions. You will meet all sorts of different mothers in the stories I have chosen.

LAURIE LEE

FROM Cider with Rosie

A particularly satisfactory mother is remembered by
the poet, Laurie Lee. In this extract she talks about her
girlhood:

*   *   *

When her brothers were big enough to look after
themselves, Mother went into domestic service. Wearing
her best straw hat and carrying a rope-tied box, seventeen
and shapely, half-wistful, half-excited, she set out alone for
that world of great houses which in those days absorbed
most of her kind. As scullery-maid, housemaid, nursemaid,
parlour-maid, in large manors all over the west, she saw
luxuries and refinements she could never forget, and to
which in some ways she naturally belonged.

The idea of the Gentry, like love or the theatre, stayed
to haunt her for the rest of her life. It haunted us too,
through her. 'Real Gentry wouldn't hear of it,' she used to
say; 'the Gentry always do it like this.' Her tone of voice,
when referring to their ways, was reverent, genteel, and
longing. It proclaimed standards of culture we could never
hope to attain and mourned their impossible perfections.

Sometimes, for instance, faced by a scratch meal in the
kitchen, Mother would transform it in a trance of memory.
A gleam would come to her hazy eyes and a special stance
to her body. Lightly she would deploy a few plates on the
table and curl her fingers airily . . .

71

'For dining, they'd have every place just *so*; personal cruets for every guest . . .' Grimly we settled to our greens and bacon: there was no way to stop her now. 'The silver and napery must be arranged in order, a set for each separate dish . . .' Our old bent forks would be whisked into line, helter-skelter along the table. 'First of all, the butler would bring in the soup (scoop-scoop) and begin by serving the ladies. There'd be river-trout next, or fresh salmon (flick-flick) lightly sprinkled with herbs and sauces. Then some woodcock perhaps, or a guinea-fowl – oh, yes, and a joint as well. And a cold ham on the sideboard, too, if you wished. For the gentlemen only, of course. The ladies never did more than pick at their food –' 'Why not?' '– Oh, it wasn't thought proper. Then Cook would send in some violet cakes, and there'd be walnuts and fruit in brandy. You'd have wine, of course, with every dish, each served in a different glass . . .' Stunned, we would listen, grinding our teeth and swallowing our empty hungers. Meanwhile Mother would have completely forgotten our soup, which then boiled over, and put out the fire.

How did Mother fit into all this, I wonder? And those neat-fingered parlour-queens, prim over-housemaids, reigning Cooks, raging Nannies, who ordered her labours – what could they have made of her? Mischievous, muddle-headed, full of brilliant fancies, half witless, half touched with wonder; she was something entirely beyond their ken and must often have been their despair. But she was popular in those halls, a kind of mascot or clown; and she was beautiful, most beautiful at that time. She may not have known it, but her pictures reveal it; she herself seemed astonished to be noticed.

Two of her stories which reflect this astonishment I remember very well. Each is no more than an incident, but when she told them to us they took on a poignancy which prevented us from thinking them stale. I must have heard them many times, right on into her later years, but at each re-telling she flushed and shone, and looked down at her hands in amazement, recalling again those two magic encounters which raised her for a moment from Annie Light the housemaid to a throne of enamelled myrtles.

The first one took place at the end of the century, when Mother was at Gaviston Court. 'It was an old house, you know; very rambling and dark; a bit primitive too in some ways. But they entertained a lot – not just Gentry, but all sorts, even black men too at times. The Master had travelled all round the world and he was a very distinguished gentleman. You never quite knew what you were going to run into – it bothered us girls at times.

'Well, one winter's night they had this big house-party and the place was packed right out. It was much too cold to use the outside privy, but there was one just along the passage. The staff wasn't supposed to use it, of course; but I thought, oh, I'll take a chance. Well, I'd just got me hand on the privy door when suddenly it flew wide open. And there, large as life, stood an Indian prince, with a turban, and jewels in his beard. I felt awful, you know – I was only a girl – I wished the ground to swallow me up. I just bobbed him a curtsy and said, "Pardon, your Highness" – I was paralysed, you see. But he only smiled, and then folded his hands, and bowed low, and said "Please madame to enter." So I held up my head, and went in, and sat down. Just like that. I felt like a Queen . . .'

The second encounter Mother always described as though it had never happened – in that special, morning, dream-telling voice that set it apart from all ordinary life. 'I was working at the time in a big red house at a place called Farnhamsurrey. On my Sundays off I used to go into Aldershot to visit my friend Amy Frost – Amy Hawkins that was, from Churchdown you know, before she got married, that is. Well, this particular Sunday I'd dressed up as usual, and I do think I looked a picture. I'd my smart lace-up boots, striped blouse and choker, a new bonnet, and crochet-work gloves. I got into Aldershot far too early so I just walked about for a bit. We'd had rain in the night and the streets were shining, and I was standing quite alone on the pavement. When suddenly round the corner, without any warning, marched a full-dress regiment of soldiers. I stood transfixed; all those men and just me; I didn't know where to look. The officer in front – he had beautiful whiskers – raised his sword and cried out "Eyes right!" Then, would you believe, the drums started rolling, and the bagpipes started to play, and all those wonderful lads as they went swinging by snapped to attention and looked straight in my eyes. I stood all alone in my Sunday dress, it quite took my breath away. All those drums and pipes, and that salute just for me – I just cried, it was so exciting . . .'

Distracted the Mother Said
to Her Boy

Distracted the mother said to her boy,
'Do you try to upset and perplex and annoy?
Now, give me four reasons – and don't play the fool –
Why you shouldn't get up and get ready for school.'

Her son replied slowly, 'Well, mother, you see,
I can't stand the teachers and they detest me;
And there isn't a boy or a girl in the place
That I like or, in turn, that delights in my face.'

'And I'll give you two reasons,' she said, 'why you ought
 Get yourself off to school before you get caught;
 Because, first, you are forty, and, next, you young fool,
 It's your job to be there.
 You're the head of the school.'

Gregory Harrison

BEVERLY CLEARY

FROM Ramona and Her Mother

There are several books about Ramona, but in this one her mother proves that she knows just how to deal with her in a crisis.

*   *   *

Ramona made up her mind to shock her parents, really shock them. 'I am going to run away,' she announced.

'I'm sorry to hear that,' said Mr Quimby as if running away were a perfectly natural thing to do.

'When are you leaving?' enquired Ramona's mother politely. The question was almost more than Ramona could bear. Her mother was supposed to say, Oh, Ramona, please, please don't leave me!

'Today,' Ramona managed to say with quivering lips. 'This morning.'

'She just wants you to feel sorry for her,' said heartless Beezus. 'She wants you to stop her.'

Ramona waited for her mother or father to say something, but neither spoke. Finally there was nothing for Ramona to do but get up from the couch. 'I guess I'll go pack,' she said, and started slowly towards her room.

No one tried to prevent her. When she reached her room, tears began to fall. She got out her Q-tip box with all her money, forty-three cents, in it. Still no one came to

76

beg her not to leave. She looked around for something in which to pack, but all she could find was an old doll's nursing kit. Ramona unzipped it and placed her Q-tip box inside. She added her best box of crayons and a pair of clean socks. Outside she heard the cheerful *ching-chong, ching-chong* of roller skates on cement. Some children were happy.

If nobody stopped her, where would she run to? Not Howie's house, even though Howie was no longer mad at her. His grandmother was not paid to look after her on Saturday. She could take the bus to Aunt Beatrice's apartment house, but Aunt Beatrice would bring her back home. Maybe she could live in the park and sleep under the bushes in the cold. Poor little Ramona, all alone in the park, shivering in the dark. Well, at least it was not raining. That was something. And there were no big wild animals, just chipmunks.

She heard her mother coming down the hall. Tears stopped. Ramona was about to be rescued. Now her mother would say, Please don't run away. We love you and want you to stay.

Instead Mrs Quimby walked into the bedroom with a suitcase in one hand and two bananas in the other. 'You will need something to pack in,' she told Ramona. 'Let me help.' She opened the suitcase on the unmade bed and placed the bananas inside. 'In case you get hungry,' she explained.

Ramona was too shocked to say anything. Mothers weren't supposed to help their children run away. 'You'll need your roller skates in case you want to travel fast,' said Mrs Quimby. 'Where are they?'

As if she were walking in her sleep, Ramona pulled her roller skates from a jumble of toys in the bottom of her closet and handed them to her mother, who placed them at

the bottom of the suitcase. How could her mother not love
a little girl like Ramona?

'Always pack heavy things at the bottom,' advised Mrs
Quimby. 'Now where are your boots in case it rains?' She
looked around the room. 'And don't forget your Betsy
book. And your little box of baby teeth. You wouldn't
want to leave your teeth behind.'

Ramona felt she could run away without her old baby teeth, and she was hurt that her mother did not want to keep them to remember her by. She stood watching while her mother packed briskly and efficiently.

'You will want Ella Funt in case you get lonely,' said Mrs Quimby.

When Ramona said her mother did not love her, she had no idea her mother would do a terrible thing like this. And her father. Didn't he care either? Apparently not. He was too busy scrubbing the bathroom to care that Ramona was in despair. And what about Beezus? She was probably secretly glad Ramona was going to run away because she could have her parents all to herself. Even Picky-picky would be glad to see the last of her.

As Ramona watched her mother fold underwear for her to take away, she began to understand that deep down inside the place where her secret thoughts were hidden, she had never really doubted her mother's love for her. Not until now . . . She thought of all the things her mother had done for her, the way she had sat up most of the night when Ramona had an earache, the birthday cake she had made in the shape of a cowboy boot all frosted with chocolate with lines of white icing that looked like stitching. That was the year she was four and had wanted cowboy boots more than anything, and her parents had given her real ones as well. She thought of the way her mother reminded her to brush her teeth. Her mother would not do that unless she cared about her teeth, would she? She thought of the time her mother let her get her hair cut at the beauty school, even though they had to scrimp and pinch. She thought of the gentle books about bears and bunnies her mother had read at bedtime when she was little.

'There.' Mrs Quimby closed the suitcase, snapped the

latches, and set it on the floor. 'Now you are all packed.'
She sat down on the bed.

Ramona pulled her car coat out of the closet and slowly
put it on, one arm and then the other. She looked at her
mother with sad eyes as she grasped the handle of her
suitcase and lifted. The suitcase would not budge. Ramona
grasped it with both hands. Still she could not lift it.

Hope flowed into Ramona's heart. Had her mother
made the suitcase too heavy on purpose? She looked
closely at her mother, who was watching her. She saw –
didn't she? – a tiny smile in her mother's eyes.

'You tricked me!' cried Ramona. 'You made the suitcase
too heavy on purpose. You don't want me to run away!'

'I couldn't get along without my Ramona,' said
Ramona's mother. She held out her arms. Ramona ran into
them. Her mother had said the words she had longed to
hear. Her mother could not get along without her. She felt
warm and safe and comforted and oh, how good her
mother smelled, so clean and sweet like flowers. Better
than any mother in the whole world. Ramona's tears
dampened her mother's blouse. After a moment Mrs
Quimby handed Ramona a Kleenex. When Ramona had
wiped her eyes and nose, she was surprised to discover that
her mother had tears in her eyes, too.

'Mama,' said Ramona, using a word she had given up as
babyish, 'why did you do that?'

'Because I could see I couldn't get anyplace arguing
with you,' answered her mother. 'You wouldn't listen.'

Kids

'Sit up straight,'
Said Mum to Mabel.
'Keep your elbows
Off the table.
Do not eat peas
Off a fork.
Your mouth is full –
Don't try and talk.
Keep your mouth shut
When you eat.
Keep still or you'll
Fall off your seat.
If you want more,
You will say "please".
Don't fiddle with
That piece of cheese!'
If then we kids
Cause such a fuss,
Why do you go on
Having us?

Spike Milligan

MICHELLE MAGORIAN

FROM Goodnight Mister Tom

One truly dreadful mother is Mrs Beech. It is wartime. Tom has just come home from being evacuated to the country, and Mrs Beech has promised him a surprise.

*   *   *

Mrs Beech led Willie round the back of their street. She told him to hide in an alleyway and watch their front door. As soon as she had opened it and coughed he was to run in. It was a strange game, thought Willie. He slid his hand into his shorts pocket and felt Zach's poem. It helped him feel less unreal.

He had not been standing long when he heard the cough. Picking up the rucksack and bags he dragged them across the pavement. His mother whispered angrily to him to hurry up. She was frightened. She didn't want anyone in the street to know that he was back. He stumbled into the front room which was still in darkness. There was a strong dank smell coming from somewhere. It was as if an animal had opened its bowels or peed somewhere.

'Is it a dog?' he asked.

'Is what a dog?'

'The surprise.'

'What surprise? Oh that. No, it's not a dog.'

She turned the light on.

The room was darker than Willie had remembered. He

stared up at the grey walls. There were two prayer books on the mantelpiece, and one on the small sideboard, still in the same position. In addition to the newspaper over the windows, it was also criss-crossed with brown tape.

'What's that for?' he asked.

'What have I said about asking questions!' she shouted, slamming her hand angrily on the table.

'Don't,' said Willie, startled.

'Are you telling me not to . . .'

'No,' interrupted Willie. 'I meant, don't ask questions. That's what you say. You say I mustn't ask questions.'

'And don't interrupt me when I'm speakin'.'

They stood, yet again, another awkward silence between them.

Willie turned away from her and then he saw it. A wooden box on a chair in the corner. He was about to ask what it was but changed his mind, walked over to it and looked inside.

'That's the surprise,' she said.

He put his hand inside.

'A baby,' he whispered. 'But why?' He stopped and turned: 'It's got tape on its mouth.'

'I know that. I didn't want her to make a noise while I was out. It's a secret, you see.'

'Ours.'

'A present?'

'Yes.'

'Who from?'

'Jesus.'

He glanced down at the baby. She was very smelly. She opened her eyes and began to cry.

'I'll pick her up,' he said, leaning towards her.

'Don't you dare.'

'But she's cryin'.'

'She's just trying to get attention. She must learn a little discipline.'

'But, but,' he stammered, 'she's only a baby.'

'Sit down!' she yelled. 'Immediately.'

Willie sat at the table.

'Has she a name?'

She brought her fist down hard on the table.

'No! And that's enough questions from you or you'll feel the belt round you.'

Willie flushed. The belt! It was still at Mister Tom's. He'd keep his mouth shut. Maybe she'd forget.

'Now let's see what you've got in those bags. And take that coat off.'

He hung it on the back of the chair, stuffing his balaclava and gloves into the pockets. He emptied the carrier bag first. He took out his old plimsolls with the tops cut off.

'They got too small,' he explained and placed his thin grey jersey, shorts, cap, mackintosh and Bible on the table beside them.

'I see you've still got your Bible,' she said. 'You've been keeping up with it, I hope, and learning it.'

'Yes, Mum.'

She leant back in her chair.

'Recite Exodus Chapter one, verses one to six.'

Willie stared at her blankly.

'I don't learn them by rote, Mum. I learns the stories like. I can tell you lots of stories, Old and New Testament.'

'I'm not interested in stories. You learnt by rote before you left here.'

'That's because I listened to the others say it in Sundee School,' he explained. 'We didn't . . .'

'Undo that other bag.'

He unfastened the straps of the rucksack and slowly

began to pull everything out. It felt as though he was stripping naked in front of her. All the things that were precious and important to him were now being placed under her scrutiny.

She sat ashen-faced and watched him unpack. When he had finished she spoke in a quiet and controlled manner.

'Now I'll ask the questions and you'll give me the answers and no back chat. Where did you get them clothes and boots you're wearin'?'

'Mr Oakley and Mrs Fletcher.'

'You steal them?'

'No. They were presents.'

'You begged.'

'No, I never.'

'Don't argue. I said you begged.'

He took hold of the eggs, fruit-cake, wine and bed-socks and slid them across to her.

'Those are your presents,' he said.

'You begged those too, I suppose.'

'No. I've got a present of me own for you,' he added. It seemed spoilt now. His surprise. It had been Mister Tom's idea. He picked up two pieces of cardboard that were strung neatly together and untied them. Inside was a drawing. It was of the graveyard and the church with fields and trees in the background. He passed it to her.

'It's where I lived.'

She looked at it.

'You steal this?'

'No.'

Now she would be pleased with him, he thought.

'No. I drew it meself.'

She looked at him coldly.

'Don't lie to me.'

'I'm not. I did it meself. Look!' and he grabbed a sketchpad that was full of drawings.

'These are mine, too,' he said, flicking over the first page.

'I haven't time to look at pictures, Willie.'

'But I did them meself!' he cried. 'Please look at them.'

'Willie. You have got a lot to learn. I shall either burn these or give them to charity. I only hope that no one ever finds out what you've done.'

Willie stared at her in dismay.

'I didn't steal them, honest, Mum. I did them. I can show you.'

'That's enough!' she said, banging her fist on the table again.

The situation was worse than she had ever imagined. It would take a lot of hard work to silence him into obedience.

'And these?' she asked, indicating the books and sweets, coloured pencils and clothes.

'Presents,' he mumbled.

'More presents, Willie? Do you expect me to believe that? Do you expect me to believe that strangers would give you presents?'

'They ent strangers, Mum. They're friends.'

'Friends! I'd like to know who these so-called friends are.'

'George and Zach and the twins and . . .'

'Are they church-goers?'

'Oh yes. George is in the choir. So am I.' His face fell. 'Was. But Ginnie and Carrie . . .'

'Girls?'

'Yes. The twins are girls. Carrie's working for . . .'

'You play with girls. After all I've said about that, and you mix with girls.'

'But they'se fine and they goes to church. They all does, all except Zach.'

'Jack? Who's he?'

'Zach,' he said. 'Short for . . .' and he bit his lip. Some instinct told him that he was approaching dangerous ground. His ears buzzed and his mother's voice began to sound distant.

'Why doesn't he go to church?' he heard her say.

He tried to evade the question.

'He believes in God, Mum, and he knows his Bible real good.'

'Why doesn't he go to church?'

'They ent got one of his sort in the village, see, and anyway' – he faltered for a second – 'he thinks that there's more God in the fields and sky and in loving people than in churches and synagogues.'

'In what?' she asked.

'In fields and,' he hesitated, 'and . . . and . . . the sky.'

'No. You said than in churches or what? What did you say?'

'Synagogues,' said Willie. 'That's what they call their churches.'

'Who?'

'Jews. Zach's Jewish.'

His mother let out a frightened scream.

'You've been poisoned by the devil! Don't you know that?' and she rose and hit him savagely across the face. He put up his hands to defend himself which only increased her anger. He reeled backwards in the chair and crashed on to the floor.

'But,' he stammered. 'Zach ses Jesus was a Jew.'

'You blasphemer!' she screamed. 'You blasphemer!'

Something heavy hit him across the head and he sank into a cold darkness. He could still hear her screaming and he knew that she was hitting him but he felt numb and separated from himself. He had become two people and one of his selves was hovering above him watching what was happening to his body.

He woke up with a jerk, shivering with the cold. He began to stretch his cramped legs but they hurt. Opening his eyes he looked around in the darkness. He knew immediately where he was. He had been locked under the stairs. He peered through the crack at the side of the small door. It was pitch black. His mother must have gone to bed. He shivered. His boots were gone, so were his jersey and shorts. He tugged at his waist and winced as he contacted a bruise. His vest had been sewn to his underpants. He took hold of the thin piece of material that lay under his body and wrapped it round himself. He could smell blood. He touched his head and discovered several painful lumps. His legs were sore and covered in something wet and congealed.

The night before, he had been lying in his first and only bed, in his first and only room. He was glad that he had left his paints and brushes there. Mister Tom would take care of them. Mister Tom! He had given him some stamped, addressed envelopes so that he could send him letters. He had also sewn two half-crowns into his overcoat. Would they still be there? Or would his mother sell the coat together with his clothes? He thought of the baby with the tape over its mouth. Maybe if she did sell them it would help the baby. He remembered the books and Zach's poem. She would certainly burn that, since it had Zach's name on it.

He felt as though he was a different person lying there in the dark. He was no longer Willie. It was as if he had said good-bye to an old part of himself. Neither was he two separate people. He was Will inside and out.

For an instant he wished he had never gone to Little

Weirwold. Then he would have thought his Mum was kind and loving. He wouldn't have known any different. A wave of despair swept through him and he cursed his new awareness. He hadn't been used to this pain for a long time. He had softened.

'Mister Tom,' he whispered in the darkness. 'Mister Tom. I want you, Mister Tom,' and he gave a quiet sob. His ankle hurt. He must have twisted it when he fell. He placed his hand round it. It was swollen and painful to touch. He let go of it and curled himself tightly into a frozen ball praying that soon he would fall asleep.

I'm Waiting for My Mum
FROM Platform

I'm waiting for my mum.
I go and stand by the
glass case on the wall
where the Christian Science people
put a Bible for you to read.
It's open and there are bits
of the page marked that you're
supposed to read.
I don't understand it.

I watch the woman in the sweety kiosk
serving people.
Mars Bar, bar of plain chocolate,
packet of chewing gum, Mars Bar, Kit Kat,
barley sugars.

Are you waiting for your mum again?

Yes.

I go and stand on the shiny floor of the waiting room
and look at the big dark benches. There's a
boiler in there.
They never light it.
Even in winter.
There are big advertisements that I read.

One says:
'Children's shoes have far to go.'
And a boy and girl are walking away
down a long long road to nowhere
with thick woods on both sides of them.
I'm not waiting for a train
I'm waiting for my mum.

Michael Rosen

PATRICIA MACLACHLAN

from Sarah, Plain and Tall

Sometimes children may have to start with a brand-new mother, as Anna and Caleb did when their father advertised for one after their own mother died.

*   *   *

Papa might not have told us about Sarah that night if Caleb hadn't asked him the question. After the dishes were cleared and washed and Papa was filling the tin pail with ashes, Caleb spoke up. It wasn't a question, really.

'You don't sing any more,' he said. He said it harshly. Not because he meant to, but because he had been thinking of it for so long. 'Why?' he asked more gently.

Slowly Papa straightened up. There was a long silence, and the dogs looked up, wondering at it.

'I've forgotten the old songs,' said Papa quietly. He sat down. 'But maybe there's a way to remember them.' He looked up at us.

'How?' asked Caleb eagerly.

Papa leaned back in the chair. 'I've placed an advertisement in the newspapers. For help.'

'You mean a housekeeper?' I asked, surprised.

Caleb and I looked at each other and burst out laughing, remembering Hilly, our old housekeeper. She was round and slow and shuffling. She snored in a high whistle at night, like a tea-kettle, and let the fire go out.

'No,' said Papa slowly. 'Not a housekeeper.' He paused.
'A wife.'

Caleb stared at Papa. 'A wife? You mean a mother?'

Nick slid his face on to Papa's lap and Papa stroked his
ears.

'That, too,' said Papa. 'Like Maggie.'

Matthew, our neighbour to the south, had written to ask
for a wife and mother for his children. And Maggie had
come from Tennessee. Her hair was the colour of turnips
and she laughed.

Papa reached into his pocket and unfolded a letter written on white paper. 'And I have received an answer.' Papa read to us:

'Dear Mr Jacob Witting,

'I am Sarah Wheaton from Maine as you will see from my letter. I am answering your advertisement. I have never been married, though I have been asked. I have lived with an older brother, William, who is about to be married. His wife-to-be is young and energetic.

'I have always loved to live by the sea, but at this time I feel a move is necessary. And the truth is, the sea is as far east as I can go. My choice, as you can see, is limited. This should not be taken as an insult. I am strong and I work hard and I am willing to travel. But I am not mild mannered. If you should still care to write, I would be interested in your children and about where you live. And you.

'Very truly yours,

'Sarah Elisabeth Wheaton

'P.S. Do you have opinions on cats? I have one.'

No one spoke when Papa finished the letter. He kept looking at it in his hands, reading it over to himself. Finally I turned my head a bit to sneak a look at Caleb. He was smiling. I smiled, too.

'One thing,' I said in the quiet of the room.

'What's that?' asked Papa, looking up.

I put my arm around Caleb.

'Ask her if she sings,' I said.

MARY RODGERS

FROM Freaky Friday

I suppose Annabel isn't really qualified to be called a
Mother, but in this story she wakes up one morning
to discover that she and her long-suffering mother
have swapped roles. Annabel still *thinks* like herself,
and nearly gets caught out as this breakfast scene
shows. It's even more complicated when she gets to
school!

*   *   *

Breakfast went off not too badly, considering it was my
first. Luckily, Daddy asked for fried (I learned how to do
that a couple of years ago) so I made fried, and toast. I
also made a small mistake.

'Sorry about the instant, Daddy, but we're all out of
regular,' I said, giving him a nice friendly kiss on the
cheek.

'*Daddy*! Since when did you start calling me Daddy? You
never did that before,' he said.

'No, and I won't again, Bill, dear,' I said, relieved at
least that he wasn't going to make a scene about the coffee.
I ran back into the kitchen to find out what Ape Face
wanted.

'What'll it be for you, lover boy?' I asked, crossing my
arms and giving him the hairy eyeball. Just watch him ask
for scrambled!

'Could I have scrambled, Mommy, please?' What did I tell you!

'No, you can't,' I said, very briskly. 'I don't have time to wash two pans. It's fried or nothing.'

'But I don't like fried,' he said. (You know, she spoils him rotten, but not me!)

'Then eat cold cereal,' I said, slapping down a box of Sugar Coated Snappy Krackles in front of him.

'But these are Annabel's. She bought them with her own money to eat when she watches television. She'll kill me if I eat up her cereal,' he said anxiously. What a worrywart.

'Listen, Ben,' I said very slowly and carefully. 'Annabel *wants* you to eat her Sugar Coated Snappy Krackles. So eat'em. NOW!' He jumped and started to eat.

Speaking of Annabel reminded me that I hadn't seen myself yet and she was going to be late for school if she didn't hurry. Me, she, I, her? I was getting very mixed up. I also wondered, as I stood outside the door to her room, what – who – I was going to find in there. Was it going to be Annabel's body with Annabel's mind in it, but I wouldn't know what the mind was thinking? Or was it going to be Annabel's body with Ma's mind in it, which would certainly be a more tidy arrangement?

Whoever-it-was was lying on her stomach on the bed, waving her feet in the air and reading a comic book. It certainly looked like Annabel. It looked like her room, too. There were all kinds of clothes dribbling out of drawers and hanging around on the floor. And one sneaker hanging around on a lamp.

'Uh, hi there,' I said cautiously.

'Phloomph,' it said. It seemed to be eating something.

'How about a nice hot cup of instant?' I suggested.

With that, whoever-it-was sat up in a hurry, turned around, and stared at me with its mouth wide open. It had not swallowed what was in its mouth. A marsh-mallow. Since I have never in my entire life seen my mother eating a marsh-mallow, I began to have a sneaking hunch that this was not my mother. It gulped and swallowed.

'A nice hot cup of *instant*?' it repeated. 'What are you? Crazy? You know I don't drink that stuff.'

It was Annabel all right. No doubt about it. Outside of the fact that Ma doesn't eat marsh-mallows and I do, there is the fact that if it was really Ma, she wouldn't ask me if I was crazy because she'd know I was Annabel thinking she was Ma. But if *she* was really Annabel too, no wonder she thought I was crazy. Any mother who asks her daughter if she wants a nice hot cup of instant has to be crazy.

'I was talking about a nice hot cup of instant oatmeal,' I said in my haughtiest voice, 'and I'll thank you not to eat marsh-mallows before breakfast. It spoils your appetite.'

'What appetite?' she said. 'I never have any appetite for all that vomitizing stuff you pile into me. Besides, I'm full up on marsh-mallows.' She patted her stomach.

I decided to give in because it was getting too late to argue.

'OK, Annabel, forget breakfast, just get yourself dressed.'

'But I can't get dressed,' she complained. 'I can't get dressed 'til I find my blue tights and I don't see where they are.' I didn't see where they were either but I found some red ones in between Book B and Book S of the Junior Britannica. (In my library, S comes after B and L follows that.)

'Why don't you wear red? Red would be nice,' I suggested in Ma's most reasonable voice. I should have known better.

'No,' she said, crossly, 'I want blue.' I looked around wildly, trying to remember where I'd put them last night. They were in the wastebasket.

'You are a living doll,' she said, blowing me several ballerina kisses. 'How can I possibly sank you for zis enormous favour you do for me?' She'd gone into her French routine. What a nut! At least she was in a good mood again. The thing about Annabel is that she usually changes her moods quickly and often. Today, I wasn't going to know what to expect, or when. What was going on in her head right now, I wondered. Maybe she was thinking about her homework and McGuirk the Jerk. If she wasn't, she should be!

'Annabel, what are you going to tell Miss McGuirk?' I asked.

'About what?' she said.

'About the English composition,' I said.

'You mean the English composition I was behind on?' she asked.

'Uh-huh,' I said.

'Oh, I handed that in early last week,' she said, looking me right in the eye. You want somebody to believe you, you always look 'em right in the eye. It's a slick trick of mine . . . works every time.

'Good girl,' I said, because that's what Ma would've said. And anyway, what did I care what went on in school? That was her problem, not mine.

Ape Face stood in the doorway, jacket on, earmuffs on, and a big, gooney smile all over his dumb face. Every day he's ready ahead of time, just to show me up, the fink!

'I'm all ready, Mommy, and I walked Max,' he said in his dumb voice. 'He did a big thing and two little things. Annabel better hurry or we're going to miss the bus.'

'If we do, it's because you're standing in my way,' she snarled. 'Get out of here, Ape Face, and don't talk to me.'

'I wasn't.'

'You are now! And don't!' she said, throwing on the rest of her clothes.

'I'm not!' he said.

'Ape Face, *shut up*!' she said. To tell the truth, both of them were getting on my nerves. I tried to remember what Ma did with us in the morning.

'All right, all right, all right, you two, that's enough of that,' I said, pushing them to the front door. So far, so good.

'And Annabel, I've told you a million times, don't call him Ape Face; his name is Ben.' Even better! I was beginning to sound more like Ma than Ma does.

'Bye-bye, darlings, have a nice day,' I said, holding the door open for them. But Ape Face just stood there. What was he waiting for, I wondered? Then a grotesque thought came to me. He was waiting to be kissed and I was going to have to do it. So I did – as quickly as possible. Actually, it wasn't too bad. He smelled kind of nice. But I hoped he didn't expect it again at lunchtime. Annabel didn't expect it at all, she never does. Just as well. I would have felt funny kissing myself good-bye.

Who?

'Who,' asked my mother,
'helped themselves to the *new* loaf?'
   My two friends and I
   looked at her
   and shrugged.

'Who,' questioned my mother,
'broke off the crust?'
   Three pairs of eyes
   stared at the loaf
   lying on the kitchen table.

'Who,' demanded my mother,
'ate the bread?'
   No one replied.
   You could hear
   the kitchen clock, Tick, Tock.

And
even now I can taste it,
crisp, fresh, warm from the bakery,
   and I'd eat it again
   if I could find a loaf
   like that, like that . . .

Wes Magee

LORD BYRON

Aged Fifteen, Writing to His Mother
From School

Harrow-on-the-Hill,
Sunday 1st May 1803

My dear Mother,

I received your Letter the other day. And am happy to hear you are well. I hope you will find Newstead in as favorable a state as you can wish. I wish you would write to Sheldrake to tell him to make haste with my shoes.

I am sorry to say that Mr Henry Drury has behaved himself to me in a manner I neither <u>can</u> nor <u>will bear</u>. He has seized now an opportunity of showing his resentment towards me. To-day in church I was talking to a Boy who was sitting next to me; that perhaps was not right, but hear what followed. After Church he spoke not a word to me, but he took this Boy to his pupil room, where he abused me in a most violent manner, called me a <u>blackguard</u>, said he <u>would</u> and <u>could</u> have me expelled from the School, and bade me thank his <u>charity</u> that <u>prevented</u> him; this was the Message he sent me, to which I shall return no answer, but submit my case to <u>you</u> and those you may think <u>fit</u> to <u>consult</u>.

Is this fit usage for anybody! had I stole or behaved in the most <u>abominable</u> way to him, his language could not have been more outrageous. What must the boys think of me to hear such a Message ordered to be delivered to me by a <u>Master</u>? Better let him take away my life than ruin my <u>Character</u>. My Conscience acquits me of ever <u>meriting</u> expulsion at this School; I have been <u>idle</u> and I certainly ought not to talk in Church, but I have never done a mean action at this School to him or <u>any one</u>. If I had done anything so <u>heinous</u>, why should he allow me to stay at the School? Why should he himself be so <u>criminal</u> as to overlook faults which merit the <u>appellation</u> of a <u>blackguard</u>? If he had it in his power to have me expelled, he would long ago have <u>done</u> it; as it is he has done <u>worse</u>. If I am treated in this Manner, I will not stay at this <u>School</u>.

I write you that I will not as yet appeal to Dr. Drury; his son's influence is more than mine and <u>justice</u> would be <u>refused</u> me. Remember I told you, when I <u>left</u> you at <u>Bath</u>, that he would seize every means and opportunity of revenge, not for leaving him so much as the mortification he suffered, because I begged you to let me leave him. If I had been the Blackguard he talks of, why did he not of his own accord refuse to keep me as his <u>pupil</u>? You know Dr. Drury's first letter, in it were these Words;
'My son and Lord Byron have had some disagreements; but I hope that his future behaviour will render a change of Tutors unnecessary.'

Last time I was here but a short time, and though he endeavoured, he could find nothing to abuse me in. Among other things I forgot to tell you he said he had a great mind to expel the boy for speaking to me, and that if he ever again spoke to me he would expel him. Let me explain his meaning; he abused me, but he neither did nor can mention anything bad of me, further than what everybody else in the School has done. I fear him not; but let him explain his meaning; 'tis all I ask. I beg you will write to Dr. Drury to let him know what I have said. He has behaved to me, as also Mr Evans, very kindly. If you do not take notice of this, I will leave the School myself; but I am sure <u>you</u> will not see me <u>ill treated</u>; better that I should suffer anything than this.

I believe you will be tired by this time of reading my letter, but, if you love me, you will now show it. Pray write to me immediately. I shall ever remain,

Your affectionate Son,

Noel Byron.

P.S. Hargreaves Hanson desires his love to you and hopes you are very well. I am not in want of any money so will not ask you for any. God bless, bless you.

BARBARA WILLARD

FROM The Queen of the Pharisees' Children

Moll is a much-loved 'travelling' Mother, and she and her family are wandering through the woods towards their winter quarters when they are attacked by robbers. (Pharisees is a gypsy name for fairies.)

* * *

Delphi fell and Will was obliged to pause and help her up. Tears were now streaming down her face.

'What happen? What happen? Shalln't we hide, brother?'

'Pick your silly feet up and leave bawling! Come fast after me. I'll needs get ahead.'

'Will . . .!'

He pulled his hand from hers and began leaping up the bank towards the place where they had made their shelter. As he reached the summit he saw what seemed at first a score of strangers – movement everywhere – struggles and shouting – terrible danger . . . Then his vision cleared a little and he saw that besides Sim and Moll there were just three unknown men. One, dark, heavy, with a great black beard, had leapt on Sim's back and was shoving him to the ground. Another was tugging at the cart, pulling it away fast. The third, shouting to the others to make haste, had Brownie by the halter and was clearly waiting to get him into the shafts. Brownie, alarmed by the noise and the smell of strangers, tugged and bucked like a two-year-old.

Moll was hanging desperately on to one side of the cart, so Will threw himself at his father's attacker, pummelling and tearing at him. As Sim went down, first on one knee and then flat to the earth itself, Will sprang on the man's shoulders and hit him about the head so that he roared, and then seized him by the sides of his beard.

The man abandoned Sim, who lay prostrate, and with a great heave, shoved Will away. But now Delphi had reached them, and she ran in and kicked at the man's shins and scratched and clawed at the backs of his hands and any bit of flesh she could reach, pinching and twisting the skin at his wrists like some terrible mad little animal.

Somewhere in the background, Fairlight was clutching the baby and screaming spasmodically.

Moll suddenly left the cart and rushed towards Delphi as the man seized her and seemed about to hurl her away into the bracken like a stone or a bone or a clod of earth. Moll sprang in her turn and now it was her nails that went into action, searing down the man's face so that the blood ran sharp and red into his beard, and then grabbing towards his eyes as if she would have them out, so wild was her rage.

The instant Moll left the cart, the second man had hauled it fast down the slope and already they had practically harnessed up Brownie. Will, aching now, partly with despair, went back to the attack. This time he seized the man about the ankles and almost brought him down.

But this enemy was like old tough leather bound and stuffed into the image of a man, and Will was far too light to do him much damage. He found himself kicked away, rolling towards the gorse bushes a little below. He would never save himself from those villainous spines, and he put his arms over his head. He landed with his face against the earth and his shoulders taking the worst of the thorny branches.

He lay still, his head spinning, and tried not to sob. Behind and above him he heard a terrible clatter and shatter as Brownie, sent on his way with a wallop, tilted the cart and upset half the contents over the rough forest floor . . .

Then suddenly everything was quiet, even Fairlight. His mother was stooping over Will, then pulling him from the gorse and fondling and rocking him; he was crying after all.

'Ah my lovely boy, my lovely boy,' she murmured to him, over and over. 'You done valiant, my fine Willow.'

Now her voice was the one he loved best to hear, the voice of the Queen of the Pharisees, and he clung to her as he had not done since he was four or five years old.

'Come now,' Moll said then, 'come to your father. He do sorely need comfort.'

Sim was sitting on his heels. He looked pale as ashes but he smiled at Moll.

'Brave as a lion, my lady,' he said. 'Sweet as a fairy and grand as their queen. I were born a seventh son and fortune touched me, surelye, first time I met wi' her . . . Come now, my children and their mam, gather up all here and see how best we'll manage.'

Soon Moll had made the fire burn brighter. She had fed the baby and put him to sleep under a bramble bush. The pot was hanging and the stew was steaming. As she looked after these matters, Sim made two packs of all they had found, rolling one in the sacking cover they used for shelter, and lashing the other around with the rope which had fallen from the cart with all the rest. These, which he balanced cunningly, he slung on the yoke for easier carrying. As soon as they had eaten, they stamped out the fire and scattered the ashes so finely that none would know any man or woman or child had dallied there.

When all this was done, they turned to go. Sim had shouldered the yoke, Moll had picked up the baby. Will and Delphi each carried a pail packed full of food from their store in the underground chamber. At the last, Sim decided that they should take the golden coin Delphi had found. It was dug up from its hiding place and released from its covering, so that Moll might slip it into her bodice, where there was a slit that she had fastened with a pin – it made a little pocket between the stuff of the bodice and its lining.

Delphi stood looking around her.

'Shalln't we ever come this way again?'

'Never,' Sim answered. 'It was a place chosen and now it is cursed. See you don't look back as you go.'

FATHERS

Here's a fine collection of fathers to choose from: strict ones, like Captain Desart (who thought a good whipping was best for little boys), or Mr Gosse who was so strict he denied Edmund any Christmas pudding. Though it must be admitted that both these were Victorians, and today's villains seem in general to be unwelcome stepfathers – like *The Ogre Downstairs* or *Goggle-Eyes*. There are also some funny and eccentric ones like Mr Gilbreth who had twelve children and thought of new ways of educating them – so we'll start with him.

FRANK AND ERNESTINE GILBRETH

FROM Cheaper by the Dozen

As well as being a genius, Mr Gilbreth was a champion brick-layer and a time and motion expert, so his twelve children all had daily charts to sign for washing, brushing teeth and buttoning up their shirts (from the bottom up because it saved two seconds). But he was a jolly man, full of good surprises.

*   *   *

Dad had promised before we came to Nantucket that there would be no formal studying – no language records and no school books. He kept his promise, although we found he was always teaching us things informally, when our backs were turned.

For instance, there was the matter of the Morse code.

'I have a way to teach you the code without any studying,' he announced one day at lunch.

We said we didn't want to learn the code, that we didn't want to learn anything until school started in the autumn.

'There's no studying,' said Dad, 'and the ones who learn it first will get rewards. The ones who don't learn it are going to wish they had.'

After lunch, he got a small paint-brush and a can of black enamel, and locked himself in the lavatory, where he painted the alphabet in code on the wall.

For the next three days Dad was busy with his paint-brush, writing code over the whitewash in every room in *The Shoe*. On the ceiling in the dormitory bedrooms he wrote the alphabet together with key words, whose accents were a reminder of the code for the various letters. It went like this: A, dot-dash, a-BOUT; B, dash-dot-dot-dot, BOIS-ter-ous-ly; C, dash-dot-dash-dot, CARE-less CHILD-ren; D, dash-dot-dot, DAN-ger-ous, etc.

When you lay on your back, dozing, the words kept going through your head, and you'd find yourself saying, 'DAN-ger-ous, dash-dot-dot, DAN-ger-ous.'

He painted secret messages in code on the walls of the front porch and dining-room.

'What do they say, Daddy?' we asked him.

'Many things,' he replied mysteriously. 'Many secret things and many things of great humour.'

We went into the bedrooms and copied the code alphabet on pieces of paper. Then, referring to the paper, we started translating Dad's messages. He went right on painting, as if he were paying no attention to us, but he didn't miss a word.

'Lord, what awful puns,' said Anne. 'And this, I presume, is meant to fit into the category of "things of great humour". Listen to this one: "Bee it ever so bumble there's no place like comb."'

'And we're stung,' Ern moaned. 'We're not going to be satisfied until we translate them all. I see dash-dot-dash-dot, and I hear myself repeating CARE-less CHILD-ren. What's this one say?'

We figured it out: 'When igorots is bliss, 'tis folly to be white.' And another, by courtesy of Mr Irwin S. Cobb, 'Eat, drink and be merry for tomorrow you may diet.' And still another, which Mother made Dad paint out, 'Two maggots were fighting in dead Ernest.'

'That one is Eskimo,' said Mother. 'I won't have it in my dining-room, even in Morse code.'

'All right, boss,' Dad grinned sheepishly. 'I'll paint over it. It's already served its purpose, anyway.'

Every day or so after that, Dad would leave a piece of paper, containing a Morse code message, on the dining-room table. Translated, it might read something like this: 'The first one who figures out this secret message should look in the right-hand pocket of my linen knickers, hanging on a hook in my room. Daddy.' Or: 'Hurry up before someone beats you to it, and look in the bottom, left drawer of the sewing machine.'

In the knickers' pocket and in the drawer would be some sort of reward – a Hershey bar, a quarter, a receipt entitling the bearer to one chocolate ice-cream soda at Coffin's Drug-Store, payable by Dad on demand.

Some of the Morse code notes were false alarms. 'Hello, Live Bait. This one is on the house. No reward. But there may be a reward next time. When you finish reading this, dash off like mad so the next fellow will think you are on some hot clue. Then he'll read it, too, and you won't be the only one who got fooled. Daddy.'

As Dad had planned, we all knew the Morse code fairly well within a few weeks. Well enough, in fact, so that we could tap out messages to each other by bouncing the tip of a fork on a butter plate. When a dozen or so persons all attempt to broadcast in this manner, and all of us preferred sending to receiving, the accumulation is loud and nerve-shattering. A present-day equivalent might be reproduced if the sound-effects man on *Gangbusters* and Walter Winchell should go on the air simultaneously, before a battery of powerful amplifiers.

The wall-writing worked so well in teaching us the code

that Dad decided to use the same system to teach us astronomy. His first step was to capture our interest, and he did this by fashioning a telescope from a camera tripod and a pair of binoculars. He'd tote the contraption out into the yard on clear nights, and look at the stars, while apparently ignoring us.

We'd gather around and nudge him, and pull at his clothes, demanding that he let us look through the telescope.

'Don't bother me,' he'd say, with his nose stuck into the glasses. 'Oh, my golly, I believe those two stars are going to collide! No. Awfully close, though. Now I've got to see what the Old Beetle's up to. What a star, what a star!'

'Daddy, give us a turn,' we'd insist. 'Don't be a pig.'

Finally, with assumed reluctance, he agreed to let us look through the glasses. We could see the ring on Saturn, three moons on Jupiter, and the craters on our own moon. Dad's favourite star was Betelgeuse, the yellowish-red 'Old Beetle' in the Orion constellation. He took a personal interest in her, because some of his friends were collaborating in experiments to measure her diameter by Michelson's interferometer.

When he finally was convinced he had interested us in astronomy, Dad started a new series of wall paintings dealing with stars. On one wall he made a scale-drawing of the major planets, ranging from Little Mercury, represented by a circle about as big as a marble, to Jupiter, as big as a basket-ball. On another, he showed the planets in relation to their distances from the sun, with Mercury the closest and Neptune the farthest away – almost in the kitchen. Pluto still hadn't been discovered, which was just as well, because there really wasn't room for it.

Dr Harlew Shapley of Harvard gave Dad a hundred or more photographs of stars, nebulae and solar eclipses. Dad hung these on the wall, near the floor. He explained that if they were up any higher, at the conventional level for pictures, the smaller children wouldn't be able to see them.

There was still some wall space left, and Dad had more than enough ideas to fill it. He tacked up a piece of cross-section graph paper, which was a thousand lines long and a thousand lines wide, and thus contained exactly a million little squares.

'You hear people talk a lot about a million,' he said, 'but not many people have ever seen exactly a million things at the same time. If a man has a million dollars, he has exactly as many dollars as there are little squares on that chart.'

'Do you have a million dollars, Daddy?' Bill asked.

'No,' said Dad a little ruefully. 'I have a million children, instead. Somewhere along the line, a man has to choose between the two.'

My Dad, Your Dad

My dad's fatter than your dad,
Yes, my dad's fatter than yours:
If he eats any more he won't fit in the house,
He'll have to live out of doors.

Yes, but my dad's balder than your dad,
My dad's balder, OK,
He's only got two hairs left on his head
And both are turning grey.

Ah, but my dad's thicker than your dad,
My dad's thicker, all right.
He has to look at his watch to see
If it's noon or the middle of the night.

Yes, but my dad's more boring than your dad.
If he ever starts counting sheep
When he can't get to sleep at night, he finds
It's the sheep that go to sleep.

But my dad doesn't mind your dad.
Mine quite likes yours too.
I suppose they don't always think much of US!
That's true, I suppose, that's true.

Kit Wright

MRS MOLESWORTH

FROM 'Carrots': Just a Little Boy

Carrots is only six and a very good little boy. He really
thought he had found a sixpence and was saving it up
to buy his sister a special surprise. But his father
wouldn't listen.

*   *   *

'Papa,' Maurice said, knocking at the door, 'may I come
in? There's something I must speak to you about immediately.'

'Come in, then,' was the reply. 'Well, and what's the
matter now? Has Carrots hurt himself?' asked his father,
naturally enough, for his red-haired little son looked pitiable
in the extreme as he crept into the room after Maurice,
frightened, bewildered, and, so far as his gentle disposition
was capable of such a feeling, indignant also, all at once.

'No,' replied Maurice, pushing Carrots forward, 'he's
not hurt himself; it's worse than that. Papa,' he continued
excitedly, 'you whipped me once, when I was a little
fellow, for telling a story. I am very sorry to trouble you,
but I think it's right you should know; I am afraid you will
have to punish Carrots more severely than you punished
me, for he's done worse than tell a story.' Maurice stopped
to take breath, and looked at his father to see the effect of
his words. Carrots had stopped crying to listen to what
Maurice was saying, and there he stood, staring up with

his large brown eyes, two or three tears still struggling down his cheeks, his face smeared and red and looking very miserable. Yet he did not seem to be in the least ashamed of himself, and this somehow provoked Mott and hardened him against him.

'What's he been doing?' said their father, looking at the two boys with more amusement than anxiety, and then glancing regretfully at the newspaper which he had been comfortably reading when Mott's knock came to the door.

'He's done much worse than tell a story,' repeated Maurice, 'though for that matter he's told two or three stories too. But, papa, you know about nurse losing a half-sovereign? Well, *Carrots* had got it all the time; he took it out of nurse's purse, and hid it away in his paint-box, without telling anybody. He can't deny it, though he tried to.'

'Carrots,' said his father sternly, 'is this true?'

Carrots looked up in his father's face; that face, generally so kind and merry, was now all gloom and displeasure – why? – Carrots could not understand, and he was too frightened and miserable to collect his little wits together to try to do so. He just gave a sort of little tremble and began to cry again.

'Carrots,' repeated his father, 'is this true?'

'I don't know,' sobbed Carrots.

'No or yes, sir,' said Captain Desart, his voice growing louder and sterner – I think he really forgot that it was a poor little shrimp of six years old he was speaking to – 'no nonsense of "don't knows". Did you or did you not take nurse's half-sovereign out of her drawer and keep it for your own?'

'No,' said Carrots, 'I never took nucken out of nurse's drawer. I never did, papa, and I didn't know nurse had any sovereigns.'

'Didn't you know nurse had *lost* a half-sovereign? Carrots, how can you say so?' interrupted Mott.

'Yes, Floss told me,' said Carrots.

'And Floss hid it away in your paint-box, I suppose?' said Mott, sarcastically.

'No, Floss didn't. I hided the sixpenny my own self,' said Carrots, looking more and more puzzled.

'Hold your tongue, Maurice,' said his father, angrily. 'Go and fetch the money and the tomfool paint-box thing that you say he had it in.'

Mott did as he was told. He ran to the nursery and back as fast as he could; but, unobserved by him, Floss managed to run after him and crept into the study so quietly that her father never noticed her.

Maurice laid the old paint-box and the half-sovereign down on the table in front of his father; Captain Desart held up the little coin between his finger and thumb.

'Now,' he said, 'Carrots, look at this. Did you or did you not take this piece of money out of nurse's drawer and hide it away in your paint-box?'

Carrots stared hard at the half-sovereign.

'I did put it in my paint-box,' he said, and then he stopped.

'What for?' said his father.

'I wanted to keep it for a secret,' he replied. 'I wanted to – to –'

'*What?*' thundered Captain Desart.

'To buy something at the toy-shop with it,' sobbed Carrots.

Captain Desart sat down and looked at Mott for sympathy.

'Upon my soul,' he said, 'one could hardly believe it. A child that one would think scarcely knew the value of money! Where can he have learnt such cunning; you say you are sure he was told of nurse's having lost a half-sovereign?'

'Oh, yes,' said Mott; 'he confesses to that much himself.'

'Floss told me,' said Carrots.

'Then how can you pretend you didn't know this was nurse's – taking it out of her drawer, too,' said his father.

'I don't know. I didn't take it out of her drawer; it was 'aside Floss's doll,' said Carrots.

'He's trying to equivocate,' said his father. Then he turned to the child again, looking more determined than ever.

'Carrots,' he said, 'I must whip you for this. Do you know that I am ashamed to think you are my son? If you were a poor boy you might be put in prison for this.'

Carrots looked too bewildered to understand. 'In prison,' he repeated. 'Would the prison-man take me?'

'What does he mean?' said Captain Desart.

Floss, who had been waiting unobserved in her corner all this time, thought this a good opportunity for coming forward.

'He means the policeman,' she said. 'Oh, papa,' she went on, running up to her little brother and throwing her arms round him, the tears streaming down her face, 'oh, papa, poor little Carrots! he *doesn't* understand.'

'Where did *you* come from?' said her father, gruffly but not unkindly, for Floss was rather a favourite of his. 'What do you mean about his not understanding? Did you know about this business, Floss?'

'Oh no, papa,' said Floss, her face flushing; 'I'm too big not to understand.'

'Of course you are,' said Captain Desart; 'and Carrots is big enough, too, to understand the very plain rule that he is not to touch what does not belong to him. He was told, too, that nurse had lost a half-sovereign, and he might then have owned to having taken it and given it back, and then things would not have looked so bad. Take him up to my dressing-room, Maurice, and leave him there till I come.'

'May I go with him, papa?' said Floss very timidly.

'No,' said her father, 'you may not.'

So Mott led off poor weeping Carrots, and all the way upstairs he kept sobbing to himself, 'I never touched nurse's sovereigns. I never did. I didn't know she had any sovereigns.'

'Hold your tongue,' said Mott; 'what is the use of telling more stories about it?'

'I didn't tell stories. I said I hided the sixpenny my own self, but I never touched nurse's sovereigns; I never did.'

EDMUND GOSSE

FROM Father and Son

When Edmund Gosse, who later became a celebrated
writer, was a child he had a deeply religious father
who did not allow him to have any comforts or
entertainments. Here's what happened one Christmas
when the servants felt sorry for him.

*   *   *

On the subject of all feasts of the Church my Father
held views of an almost grotesque peculiarity. He looked
upon each of them as nugatory and worthless, but the
keeping of Christmas appeared to him by far the most hate-
ful, and nothing less than an act of idolatry. 'The
very work is Popish,' he used to exclaim, 'Christ's Mass!'
pursing up his lips with the gesture of one who tastes
assafoetida by accident. Then he would adduce the antiquity
of the so-called feast, adapted from horrible heathen
rites, and itself a soiled relic of the abominable Yule-Tide.
He would denounce the horrors of Christmas until it almost
made me blush to look at a holly-berry.

On Christmas Day of this year 1857 our villa saw a very
unusual sight. My Father had given strictest charge that no
difference whatever was to be made in our meals on that
day; the dinner was to be neither more copious than usual
nor less so. He was obeyed, but the servants, secretly
rebellious, made a small plum-pudding for themselves. (I

discovered afterwards, with pain, that Miss Marks received a slice of it in her boudoir.) Early in the afternoon, the maids, – of whom we were now advanced to keeping two, – kindly remarked that 'the poor dear child ought to have a bit, anyhow', and wheedled me into the kitchen, where I ate a slice of plum-pudding. Shortly I began to feel that pain inside which in my frail state was inevitable, and my conscience smote me violently. At length I could bear my spiritual anguish no longer, and bursting into the study I called out: 'Oh! Papa, Papa, I have eaten of flesh offered to idols!' It took some time, between my sobs, to explain what had happened. Then my Father sternly said: 'Where is the accursed thing?' I explained that as much as was left of it was still on the kitchen table. He took me by the hand, and ran with me into the midst of the startled servants, seized what remained of the pudding, and with the plate in one hand and me still tight in the other, ran till we reached the dustheap, when he flung the idolatrous confectionery on to the middle of the ashes, and then raked it deep down into the mass The suddenness, the violence, the velocity of this extraordinary act made an impression on my memory which nothing will ever efface.

ANNE FINE

FROM Goggle-Eyes

Kitty calls her mother's new friend Goggle-eyes because he's always in the house making eyes at her mother, and she's afraid he's going to take her father's place.

*   *   *

I hated having Goggle-eyes about. I hated the whole house whenever he was in it. I can't describe exactly what it was, but it just didn't feel like home any more if he was ambling from room to room in search of a pencil to do the crossword, or slipping out of the downstairs lavatory leaving the cistern hissing behind him, or lifting my schoolbag off the coffee table so he could lean back on the sofa and watch the news on the telly. I hated Mum for being happy and relaxed, and nice to him. I hated Jude simply for answering whenever he asked her a trivial little question or said something casual and friendly. And sometimes I even hated sweet furry Floss for taking advantage of the fact that Goggle-eyes wasn't the most active of men, and settling on his trouser legs to moult and purr and dribble away contentedly.

But most of all, of course, I hated him.

And he knew, too. He wasn't stupid. It can't have escaped his notice that during all the evenings he spent in our house, I never once spoke to him willingly, never began a conversation, and only answered when he spoke to me if Mum was in the room to see and hear. If she was busy on the phone or in the bathroom when he said something, I'd just pretend I hadn't heard, or I'd walk out of the room, or start to play *The Muppet Show Theme* on Jude's descant recorder as loudly as possible. It sounds rude and childish, but that's how I *felt*. Each evening I'd hear the tell-tale noise of his car engine cutting out at our kerb, and I'd glance out of the nearest window to see him heaving himself out of the driver's seat and reaching his thumbs in the waistband of his trousers to hitch them straight before he strolled up our path. The very sight of him used to annoy me so much I'd make some excuse to slip upstairs, and I might even stay there the whole of the evening, pretending to read or be doing some homework, rather than come down and be forced to be civil and friendly.

Mum saw — but didn't, if you see what I mean. Oh, she knew I wasn't exactly crazy about him. She knew I'd probably just as soon he fell under a bus, or pushed off to Papua New Guinea or Kuala Lumpur, or took up with someone else's mother instead. But I don't think she had the faintest idea how strongly I felt, how much he got on my nerves, how much I loathed him.

And I couldn't talk to her about it at all. Each time I tried, I found myself standing fishing helplessly for words, and we'd just end up with her peering into my face, a little concerned and expectant, and me saying irritably: 'Nothing! It doesn't matter, honestly. *Forget* it.'

Once, when she was out, I tried to talk to Dad, but he wasn't very helpful.

'What's *wrong* with him, sweetheart?'

I twisted the coils of green plastic telephone wire around my little finger, and pulled hard.

'He's *horrible*. That's what's wrong with him.'

'What do you mean, horrible?'

'He's slimy.'

'Slimy?'

'Yes. He's slimy and creepy and revolting. He makes me absolutely sick. I only have to glance in his direction and I want to throw up.'

'What does Jude think of him?'

There's no point in telling actual lies. They always catch you out in the end.

'Jude sort of likes him.'

There was a silence, then:

'As a matter of curiosity, what does this Gerald Faulkner look like?'

'Horrible.'

'Kitty, I bet this is nonsense. I bet this new friend of your mother's doesn't look horrible at all. I bet he looks perfectly normal – middle-aged, getting a bit thick in the middle, going a bit thin on top . . .'

He might as well have been describing himself. I expect he'd turned round to admire himself in his hall mirror.

'I suppose so.'

I pulled the plastic wire even tighter, to make the tip of my finger go blue.

'And I expect he has a normal face too, hasn't he? I mean, if people saw him coming down the street, they wouldn't shriek and scuttle up the nearest alley.'

'*I* would.'

My finger was bright purple now.

'But what's *wrong* with him?'

You could tell from the tone of his voice that he was getting as frustrated as I was with this phone call.

'Apart from the fact that he's horrible and slimy and creepy and revolting and makes me absolutely sick?'

'Yes. Apart from all that.'

'I don't know,' I wailed desperately down the telephone wire and all the way to Berwick upon Tweed. 'I just don't *know*.'

And I didn't, either. I couldn't work out what it was about Gerald Faulkner that kept me lying awake in bed imagining all those dire accidents in which I made him the star, night after night. On Monday I'd arrange for a huge industrial chimney to topple on his head. On Tuesday he'd succumb to a grisly and incurable disease. Some drunk driver might run him over on Wednesday. On Thursday he'd lose his footing strolling with Mum along the path beside the reservoir, slip in and drown. Honestly, I spent so much time thinking up fatal accidents for Goggle-eyes that sometimes when he turned up at our house on Friday with the customary box of chocolates under his arm, I'd catch myself feeling astonished he looked as fit and healthy as he did.

He'd step inside and scoop Floss up into his arms.

'Is Scotland playing Brazil tonight in your hall?' he'd ask, nodding at all the lights blazing away. 'You know, Kitty, a clever anti-nuclear campaigner like you ought to go round this house and switch off a few lights. Take the pressure off your local reactor. Make Torness redundant.'

I'd scowl. He'd smile, and stroll on past me into the living room where Jude would be waiting with the Monopoly or the Scrabble all set out ready on the coffee table. Sometimes he'd switch off a couple of lights on the way. He had a thing about wasting electricity, you could tell. Sometimes I'd catch him in the hall on his way back from the lavatory, peering at our meter, watching the little wheel spin round and round.

'You *must* have left something running,' he'd tell me anxiously. 'Perhaps your washing machine is stuck on spin. I can't *believe* it's going round this fast just for the lights!'

Jude would come out and giggle at him until he gave up his fretting, and turned round to lead her back to their game. I'd stamp upstairs to my bedroom, flicking down every single light switch I passed on the way. And down is *on* in our house – that's how much he annoyed me.

And I annoyed him, I know I did. I was a little turd, to tell the truth. I made a point of never passing on his phone messages. I pulled snide little faces whenever he spoke. I acted as if everything he brought into our house was either potentially explosive or deadly poisonous. I wouldn't come near the fabulous shell collection he brought round to show Jude when she finished with *Ancient Rome* and moved on to *The Sea Shore*, and I wouldn't be caught dead eating any of his chocolates. Oh, yes. I don't deny it. I got on his nerves as much as he got on mine.

And I was just as bad if we went out. I'd drag behind, desperately hoping that no one I knew would walk past and see him arm in arm with my mother, and think for a moment that he might be my dad.

The Reverend Sabine Baring-Gould

The Reverend Sabine Baring-Gould,
   Rector (sometime) at Lew,
Once at a Christmas party asked,
   'Whose pretty child are you?'

(The Rector's family was long,
   His memory was poor,
And as to who was who had grown
   Increasingly unsure).

At this, the infant on the stair
   Most sorrowfully sighed.
'Whose pretty little girl am I?
   Why, *yours*, papa!' she cried.

Charles Causley

Thank You, Dad, for Everything

Thank you for laying the carpet, dad,
Thank you for showing us how,
But what is that lump in the middle, dad?
And why is it saying mia-ow?

Doug MacLeod

DIANA WYNNE JONES

FROM The Ogre Downstairs

This stepfather seems to be so awful that it's hard to believe in him. He's not only bossy and unreasonable to his stepsons, Caspar and Johnny, but horrid to his own two, Malcolm and Douglas, and the two sets of boys can't bear each other.

To make matters worse, they've each been given boxes of magic tricks, which include ways to make them fly, and cause their toffee bars to multiply! It's not surprising that Sally, their mother and stepmother, disappears, and they get into a great deal of trouble.

*　　*　　*

The Ogre opened the study door and came in, with his least likeable expression on his face. 'What do you think you're doing here?' he said when he saw Gwinny. 'Get out.'

Gwinny stood up. 'Will you please tell me where Mummy is,' she said bravely.

The Ogre glowered. 'She went to your grandmother's. She needed a rest.'

'Oh,' said Gwinny. 'Did she go straight from work?'

'She did,' said the Ogre. 'Out.'

Gwinny, very straight and upright, walked past him and along the hall. She knew something was not right. And she felt heavier and more anxious than ever. The front door opened as she reached the hall. Gwinny stood still and watched Caspar, Johnny and Malcolm come in.

'Is something wrong?' Caspar said, seeing her face.

Gwinny nodded. 'Mummy's gone. The Ogre said she's gone to Granny's straight from work.'

All three looked at her in dismay. None of them were exactly surprised, remembering the expression on Sally's face the night before, and the things the Ogre had said to her. But it was odd.

'Why didn't she tell us?' Johnny said.

'I don't know,' said Gwinny. 'But I don't think the Ogre was telling the truth.'

'Why not?' said Caspar.

'Because she hasn't made her bed,' said Gwinny. 'She always does.' Johnny and Caspar looked at one another in alarm and bewilderment.

'You could check up,' Malcolm suggested. 'Is your grandmother on the phone?' He was very pale and tired-looking. Gwinny thought he might be ill.

'Are you all right?' she asked.

'Perfectly,' said Malcolm.

Caspar threw down his schoolbags and seized the address-book by the telephone. He found the number and dialled. 'Where's the Ogre?'

'Study,' said Gwinny. 'Don't talk loud.'

Granny answered the phone. 'Caspar! Well I never!' She was both surprised and delighted. 'And how are you all?'

With his stomach sinking a little, Caspar said, 'Fine, Granny. Has Mum arrived yet?'

'Your mother?' said Granny. 'No, I've not seen Sally, dear. Why?'

Caspar did not quite know what to say after this. 'Well,' he explained hesitantly, 'I thought she was supposed to be coming to see you straight from work.'

'Oh, I *see*!' cried Granny. 'Thank you for warning me, dear. Sally knows how I hate being taken by surprise. I'll go and put a cake in the oven for her. Thank you, dear. Goodbye.' Since Caspar had no idea how to explain what he meant without alarming Granny thoroughly, he was thankful when she rang off.

'Well?' asked Johnny.

'Granny didn't know she was coming. But she might just not have got there yet,' Caspar said, hoping for the best.

'Well, she ought to have done,' said Gwinny. 'Because I think she went this morning.'

'So do I, now I think about it,' said Malcolm.

They looked at one another, all thoroughly alarmed, wondering what this meant. And while they were standing in a group, staring, the front-door opened again and Douglas came in. He stopped short when he saw the look on their faces. 'What's up?' he said.

'Mummy's gone,' said Gwinny. 'And the Ogre told me a lie about where she was.'

Douglas looked as dismayed as they were, and more dismayed still as they explained. 'You have to hand it my father,' he said at length. 'He certainly has a knack of getting rid of his wives.'

The story of Bluebeard burst into Johnny's head. 'You don't think,' he said, 'that he's killed her and buried her at the end of the garden, do you?' Gwinny was horrified.

'Don't be a nit!' said Douglas. 'People don't do that.' Somehow, neither Gwinny nor Johnny was reassured by the way he said it. And, unfortunately, Caspar was too worried himself to think of backing Douglas up. So Gwinny and Johnny both gained a distinct impression that, if it had chanced to be the fashion to kill your wife and bury her at the end of the garden, Douglas would have expected the Ogre to do it. 'You see,' said Douglas, glancing at Malcolm. Then he saw how ill Malcolm was looking. 'You'd better get to bed,' he said.

'If you don't mind,' Malcolm said politely, 'I think I will.'

At that, Caspar and Johnny noticed how poorly he seemed and loudly told him not to be a fool and to go to bed at once. Malcolm went away upstairs rather gladly.

'He always gets ill if people hit him,' Douglas explained. 'I was up half the night with him and —'

'Don't *you* hit him, then?' Caspar asked, in some surprise.

'Of course not!' Douglas said irritably. 'But the point is, I think Sally may even have left last night. They had a flaming row, anyway. They were shouting at one another until gone three o'clock.'

'What about?' Johnny asked miserably.

'You, I think,' said Douglas. 'Then I heard Sally slamming round the house afterwards. And I don't think she was here this morning, whatever Father said.'

'Then where do you think she went?' said Caspar.

'Couldn't tell you for toffee, I'm afraid,' said Douglas.

Gwinny clapped her hands over her mouth. 'Oh! The toffee-bars! They're all over that radiator again. I forgot.'

'Oh, *no!*' said Johnny.

They all streamed upstairs to look. The mess was, if possible, worse now. 'Wow!' said Douglas, when he saw it.

'The ones you hid in our cupboard had babies, in case you didn't know,' Johnny told him. Caspar was too depressed to do more than give Douglas a disgusted look.

'I'm sorry,' said Douglas. 'How was I to know they'd do this? We'd better get it cleared up before the Ogre sees it.'

Nobody argued about that. Douglas fetched the fateful

bucket again. Johnny brought six face-flannels – Sally's was missing. Gwinny found soap and soda and washing-powder, and Caspar collected all the fluttering wrappers. Then they all set to work to peel the upper layers of toffee off the radiator.

The Ogre, alerted by the clattering of the bucket and the running of taps, appeared in the doorway while they were doing it. Johnny uttered a yelp of dismay. They all froze. 'Who did it this time?' said the Ogre.

Since nobody exactly *had* done it, nobody answered.

'Are you here in an organizing capacity, Douglas?' the Ogre enquired. 'Or have they corrupted you too?'

Douglas went red. 'It may surprise you to know,' he said, 'that it was at least half my fault.'

The Ogre shook his head. 'It doesn't surprise me at all. Johnny and Caspar could corrupt a saint. And I've had enough of them. I'm going to get rid of them if I can.'

'Get rid of them?' Gwinny said, quite appalled. 'Like you got rid of Mummy, you mean?'

'I *haven't* got rid of Sally,' the Ogre said irritably.

'Then what have you done with her?' demanded Caspar. 'You didn't tell Gwinny the truth, did you?'

'You lied,' said Johnny.

'Yes, whatever you did, you'd no call to lie to them,' Douglas said angrily.

The Ogre looked along their four defiant faces in the greatest surprise. He could not in the least understand why they should be so angry. It never once occurred to him that they needed to be told the truth. 'You're all being quite ridiculous,' he said. 'Sally's simply gone away for a short holiday. You wretched children had tired her out between you.'

'She hasn't gone to Granny, though,' said Caspar. 'And why didn't she tell *us*?'

'If you must know, she's gone to a hotel by the seaside,'

said the Ogre. 'And she didn't tell you because she was sick and tired of you.'

'Is that the truth this time?' Douglas demanded.

'Douglas,' said the Ogre, 'you may bully Malcolm, but you are not going to use that tone with me.' They all knew at once from this that he had not told them the truth. And, if they needed anything more to complete their hatred and distrust of him, they had it in what he said next. 'This is your fault, Caspar and Johnny,' he said. 'You two are destroying Sally's health, what with your water and your toffee and climbing on roofs, and I'm going to send you away to boarding school after Christmas to learn some decent behaviour. I've had enough of you.'

Caspar and Johnny were too appalled to speak. Douglas said, 'That's quite unfair! It's just that these two haven't learnt how not to be found out yet, and we have!'

'I take it you're asking to be sent away too?' said the Ogre.

'No fear!' said Douglas, with deep feeling.

'Then don't provoke me,' said the Ogre. 'Get this revolting mess cleaned up, and then get down to the kitchen and find something we can eat.'

Letter from a Parent

Dear Sir,
      I feel I ought to write
About Tom's essay-work last night.
Of all the subjects you have set
This seemed the most imprudent yet.
'Describe your family' . . . Tom did it,
So well, I just had to forbid it
Being handed in; – so did my wife.
The details of our family life
Are not of such a kind, alas,
That I should want them read in class:
We did not wish the High School staff
To scan them for a lunch-hour laugh.
We tore it out. I realize
You may think what we did unwise –
But give it your consideration
And please accept my explanation.
I trust you will not blame my son,
For, after all, the work *was done*.
                 Yours truly
                 Harold Honeybun

                 Kenneth Kitchin

ANNE BOLEYN

A Letter to her Father

Anne Boleyn, aged eight, to her father, Sir Thomas Boleyn before her appointment as a Maid of Honour to Mary, Queen of France, sister of King Henry VIII.

Sir,

You tell me in your letter that you want me to behave properly when I come to Court, and that the Queen will take the trouble to talk to me. I am very excited that I shall be talking to a person who is so clever and elegant. This will make me want to carry on learning to speak and write good French more than ever . . .

Sir, please excuse if this letter is badly written, because all the spelling comes out of my own head, while the other letters I just copied, and Semmonet says he has left me to write the letter by myself so that no one else knows what I'm saying to you . . .

TOVE JANSSON

FROM Moominpappa at Sea

Moomins are short and fat and shy, and live in the
forests of Finland. In this story Moominpappa is feeling left out – until he hears about a fire in the forest.

*   *   *

One afternoon at the end of August, Moominpappa was
walking about in his garden feeling at a loss. He had no
idea what to do with himself, because it seemed everything
there was to be done had already been done or was being
done by somebody else.

Moominpappa aimlessly pottered about in his garden,
his tail dragging along the ground behind him in a
melancholy way. Here, down in the valley, the heat was
scorching; everything was still and silent, and not a little
dusty. It was the month when there could be great forest
fires, the month for taking great care.

He had warned the family. Time and time again he had
explained how necessary it was to be careful in August. He
had described the burning valley, the roar of the flames,

the white-hot tree trunks, and the fire creeping along the ground underneath the moss. Blinding columns of flame flung upwards against the night sky! Waves of fire, rushing down the sides of the valley and on towards the sea . . .

'Sizzling, they throw themselves into the sea,' finished Moominpappa with gloomy satisfaction. 'Everything is black, everything has been burned up. A tremendous responsibility rests on the smallest creature who can lay his paws on matches.'

The family stopped what they were doing and said: 'Yes. Of course. Yes, yes.' Then they took no more notice of him, and got on with what they were doing.

They were always doing something. Quietly, without interruption, and with great concentration, they carried on with the hundred-and-one small things that made up their world. It was a world that was very private, and self-contained, and to which nothing could be added. Like a map where everything has been discovered, everywhere inhabited, and where there are no bare patches left any longer. And they said to each other: 'He always talks about forest fires in August.'

Moominpappa climbed up the veranda steps. His paws got stuck in the varnish as usual, making little sucking sounds all the way up and across the floor, right up to the wicker chair. His tail got stuck, too; it felt as though someone was pulling it.

Moominpappa sat down and shut his eyes. 'That floor ought to be revarnished,' he thought. 'The heat makes it like that, of course. But a good varnish shouldn't start melting just because it's hot. Perhaps I used the wrong sort of varnish. It's an awful long time since I built the veranda, and it's high time it was revarnished. But first it'll have to be rubbed with sandpaper, a rotten job that no one will thank me for doing. But there's something special about a new white floor, painted with a thick brush and shiny varnish. The family will have to use the back door and keep out of the way while I'm doing it. And then I'll let them come in, saying: "There you are! Look, your new veranda!" . . . It's much too hot. I'd love to be out sailing. Sailing right out to sea, as far as I can go . . .'

Moominpappa felt a sleepy feeling in his paws. He shook himself and lit his pipe. The match went on burning in his ash-tray, and he watched it, fascinated. Just before it went out he tore up some bits of newspaper and put them on the flame. It was a pretty little fire, hardly visible in the sunshine, but it was burning nicely. He watched it carefully.

'It's going out again,' said Little My. 'Put some more on!' She was sitting in the shade on the veranda railings.

'Oh, it's you!' said Moominpappa, and he shook the ash-tray until the fire went out. 'I'm just watching the way fire burns. It's very important.'

Little My laughed, and went on looking at him. Then he

pulled his hat down over his eyes and took refuge in sleep.

'Pappa,' said Moomintroll. 'Wake up! We've just put out a forest fire!'

Both Moominpappa's paws were stuck firmly to the floor. He wrenched them loose with a strong feeling of reluctance. It wasn't fair. 'What are you talking about?' he said.

'A real little forest fire,' Moomintroll told him. 'Just behind the tobacco-patch. The moss was on fire, and Mamma says that it might have been a spark from the chimney . . .'

Moominpappa leaped into the air and in a flash became a determined man-of-action. His hat rolled down the steps.

'We put it out!' Moomintroll shouted. 'We put it out straight away. There's nothing for you to worry about!'

Moominpappa stopped dead. He was feeling very angry. 'Have you put it out without me?' he said. 'Why didn't anybody tell me? You just let me go on sleeping without saying anything!'

'But, dearest,' said Moominmamma leaning out of the kitchen window, 'we didn't think it was really necessary to wake you up. It was a very small fire, and it was only smoking a little. I happened to be going by with some buckets of water, so all I had to do was to sprinkle a few drops on it in passing . . .'

'In passing,' cried Moominpappa. 'Just sprinkle. Sprinkle, indeed! What a word! And leaving the fire to burn under the moss unguarded! Where is it? Where is it?'

Moominmamma left what she was doing and led the way to the tobacco-patch. Moomintroll stayed on the veranda gazing after them. The black spot in the moss was a very small spot indeed.

'Don't imagine,' said Moominpappa at last, very slowly, 'that a spot like this isn't dangerous. Far from it. It can go on burning *under* the moss, you see. In the ground. Hours and perhaps even days may go by, and then suddenly, whoof! The fire breaks out somewhere quite different. Do you see what I mean?'

'Yes, dearest,' answered Moominmamma.

'So I'm going to stay here,' Moominpappa went on, sulkily digging in the moss. 'I shall stand guard over it. I'll stay here all night if necessary.'

'Do you really think,' Moominmamma began. Then she just said, 'Yes. That's very good of you. One never knows what will happen with moss.'

Moominpappa sat all the afternoon watching the little black spot, first pulling up the moss for quite a way round it. He wouldn't leave it to go indoors for his dinner. He really wanted the others to think he was offended.

'Do you think he'll stay out there all night?' asked Moomintroll.

'It's quite possible,' said Moominmamma.

'If you're sore, you're sore,' observed Little My, peeling her potatoes with her teeth. 'You have to be angry sometimes. Every little creep has a right to be angry. But Pappa's angry in the wrong way. He's not letting it out, just shutting it up inside him.'

'My dear child,' said Moominmamma, 'Pappa knows what he's doing.'

'I don't think he does,' said Little My simply. 'He doesn't know at all. Do you know?'

'Not really,' Moominmamma had to admit.

Dad's Friend, Jim

My dad has a friend
called Jim.

He comes to my house
and he asks my dad
does he want to go to the pub.

My dad says yes.

If I had friends
when I was bigger,
I would go to the pub
with them.

And have some laughs.

I would like a friend
like my dad's friend,
Jim.

Thomas Egan, 6

Daddy Fell into the Pond

Everyone grumbled. The sky was grey.
We had nothing to do and nothing to say.
We were nearing the end of a dismal day.
And there seemed to be nothing beyond,
　Then
　　Daddy fell into the pond!

And everyone's face grew merry and bright,
And Timothy danced for sheer delight.
'Give me the camera, quick, oh quick!
He's crawling out of the duckweed!' Click!

Then the gardener suddenly slapped his knee,
And doubled up, shaking silently,
And the ducks all quacked as if they were daft,
And it sounded as if the old drake laughed.
Oh, there wasn't a thing that didn't respond
　When
　　Daddy fell into the pond!

Alfred Noyes

JAMES THURBER

The Night the Bed Fell

FROM My Life and Hard Times

James Thurber grew up in Ohio, America, and in his books he describes many funny episodes from his childhood. One of my particular favourites is *The Night the Bed Fell.*

*   *   *

It happened, then, that my father had decided to sleep in the attic one night, to be away where he could think. My mother opposed the notion strongly because, she said, the old wooden bed up there was unsafe: it was wobbly and the heavy headboard would crash down on father's head in case the bed fell, and kill him. There was no dissuading him, however, and at a quarter past ten he closed the attic door behind him and went up the narrow twisting stairs. We later heard ominous creakings as he crawled into bed. Grandfather, who usually slept in the attic bed when he was with us, had disappeared some days before. (On these occasions he was usually gone six or eight days and returned growling and out of temper, with the news that the federal Union was run by a passel of blockheads and that the Army of the Potomac didn't have any more chance than a fiddler's bitch.)

We had visiting us at this time a nervous first cousin of mine named Briggs Beall, who believed that he was likely to cease breathing when he was asleep. It was his feeling that if he were not awakened every hour during the night, he might die of suffocation. He had been accustomed to setting an alarm clock to ring at intervals until morning, but I persuaded him to abandon this. He slept in my room and I told him that I was such a light sleeper that if anybody quit breathing in the same room with me, I would wake instantly. He tested me the first night – which I had suspected he would – by holding his breath after my regular breathing had convinced him I was asleep. I was not asleep, however, and called to him. This seemed to allay his fears a little, but he took the precaution of putting a glass of spirits of camphor on a little table at the head of his bed. In case I didn't arouse him until he was almost gone, he said, he would sniff the camphor, a powerful reviver . . .

By midnight we were all in bed. The layout of the rooms and the disposition of their occupants is important to an understanding of what later occurred. In the front room upstairs (just under father's attic bedroom) were my mother and my brother Herman, who sometimes sang in his sleep, usually 'Marching Through Georgia' or 'Onward, Christian Soldiers'. Briggs Beall and myself were in a room adjoining this one. My brother Roy was in a room across the hall from ours. Our bull terrier, Rex, slept in the hall.

My bed was an army cot, one of those affairs which are made wide enough to sleep on comfortably only by putting up, flat with the middle section, the two sides which ordinarily hang down like the sideboards of a drop-leaf table. When these sides are up, it is perilous to roll too far toward the edge, for then the cot is likely to tip completely over, bringing the whole bed down on top of one, with a tremendous banging crash. This, in fact, is precisely what happened, about two o'clock in the morning. (It was my mother who, in recalling the scene later, first referred to it as 'the night the bed fell on your father.')

Always a deep sleeper, slow to arouse (I had lied to Briggs), I was at first unconscious of what had happened when the iron cot rolled me on to the floor and toppled over on me. It left me still warmly bundled up and unhurt, for the bed rested above me like a canopy. Hence I did not wake up, only reached the edge of consciousness and went back. The racket, however, instantly awakened my mother, in the next room, who came to the immediate conclusion that her worst dread was realized: the big wooden bed upstairs had fallen on father. She therefore screamed, 'Let's go to your poor father!' It was this shout, rather than the noise of my cot falling, that awakened Herman, in the same room with her. He thought that mother had become, for no apparent reason, hysterical. 'You're all right, Mamma!' he shouted, trying to calm her. They exchanged shout for shout for perhaps ten seconds: 'Let's go to your poor father!' and 'You're all right!' That woke up Briggs. By this time I was conscious of what was going on, in a vague way, but did not yet realize that I was under my bed instead of on it. Briggs, awakening in the midst of loud shouts of fear and apprehension, came to the quick conclusion that he was suffocating and that we were all trying to 'bring him out'. With a low moan, he grasped the glass of camphor at the head of his bed and instead of sniffing it poured it over himself. The room reeked of camphor. 'Ugf, ahfg,' choked Briggs, like a drowning man, for he had almost succeeded in stopping his breath under the deluge of pungent spirits. He leaped out of bed and groped toward the open window, but he came up against one that was closed. With his hand, he beat out the glass, and I could hear it crash and tinkle on the alleyway below. It was at this juncture that I, in trying to get up, had the uncanny sensation of feeling my bed above me! Foggy with sleep, I now suspected, in my turn, that the whole uproar was

149

being made in a frantic endeavour to extricate me from what must be an unheard-of and perilous situation.

'Get me out of this!' I bawled. 'Get me out!' I think I had the nightmarish belief that I was entombed in a mine. 'Gugh,' gasped Briggs, floundering in his camphor.

By this time my mother, still shouting, pursued by Herman, still shouting, was trying to open the door to the attic, in order to go up and get my father's body out of the wreckage. The door was stuck, however, and wouldn't yield. Her frantic pulls on it only added to the general banging and confusion. Roy and the dog were now up, the one shouting questions, the other barking.

Father, farthest away and soundest sleeper of all, had by this time been awakened by the battering on the attic door. He decided that the house was on fire. 'I'm coming, I'm coming!' he wailed in a slow, sleepy voice – it took him many minutes to regain full consciousness. My mother, still believing he was caught under the bed, detected in his 'I'm coming!' the mournful resigned note of one who is preparing to meet his Maker. 'He's dying!' she shouted.

'I'm all right!' Briggs yelled to reassure her. 'I'm all right!' He still believed that it was his own closeness to death that was worrying mother. I found at last the light switch in my room, unlocked the door, and Briggs and I joined the others at the attic door. The dog, who never did like Briggs, jumped for him – assuming that he was the culprit in whatever was going on – and Roy had to throw Rex and hold him. We could hear father crawling out of bed upstairs. Roy pulled the attic door open, with a mighty jerk, and father came down the stairs, sleepy and irritable but safe and sound. My mother began to weep when she saw him. Rex began to howl. 'What in the name of God is going on here?' asked father.

The situation was finally put together like a gigantic

jigsaw puzzle. Father caught a cold from prowling around in his bare feet but there were no other bad results. 'I'm glad,' said mother, who always looked on the bright side of things, 'that your grandfather wasn't here.'

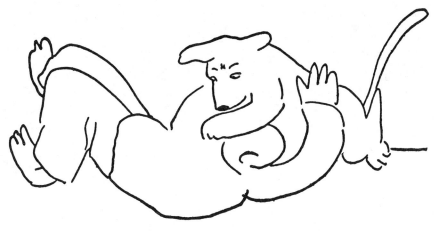

ROY HAD TO THROW REX

BROTHERS AND SISTERS

Though there are lots of good stories about brothers and sisters, I don't know any in which they are always 'like little birds agreeing in their nests', as Isaac Watts suggests they should be. On the other hand, not many sisters will quarrel as bitterly as Amy and Jo in the passage from *Little Women*. I think that most of us are probably somewhere in between.

My Sister Clarissa Spits Twice if I Kiss Her

My sister Clarissa spits twice if I kiss her
and once if I hold her hand.
I reprimand her – my name's Alexander –
for spitting I simply can't stand.

'Clarissa, Clarissa, my sister, is this a
really nice habit to practise?'
But she always replies with innocent eyes
rather softly, 'Dear Brother, the fact is

I think I'm an ape with a very small grape
crushed to juice in my mastodon lips.
Since I am not a prude, though I hate being rude,
I am simply ejecting the pips.'

George Barker

LOUISA M. ALCOTT

FROM Little Women

The four March girls, Meg, Jo, Beth and Amy, must
be the best-behaved sisters in all literature, but I think
it is more fun when they occasionally fall from
grace. Here are Jo and Amy having a really dreadful
quarrel.

*   *   *

'Girls, where are you going?' asked Amy, coming into
their room one Saturday afternoon, and finding them
getting ready to go out, with an air of secrecy, which
excited her curiosity.

'Never mind; little girls shouldn't ask questions,'
returned Jo, sharply.

Now if there *is* anything mortifying to our feelings, when
we are young, it is to be told that; and to be bidden to 'run
away, dear', is still more trying to us. Amy bridled up at this
insult, and determined to find out the secret, if she teased
for an hour. Turning to Meg, who never refused her
anything very long, she said coaxingly, 'Do tell me! I should
think you might let me go too; for Beth is fussing over her
piano, and I haven't got anything to do, and am *so* lonely.'

'I can't, dear, because you aren't invited,' began Meg;
but Jo broke in impatiently, 'Now, Meg, be quiet, or you
will spoil it all. You can't go, Amy; so don't be a baby and
whine about it.'

156

'You are going somewhere with Laurie, I know you are; you were whispering and laughing together, on the sofa, last night, and you stopped when I came in. Aren't you going with him?'

'Yes, we are; now do be still and stop bothering.'

Amy held her tongue, but used her eyes, and saw Meg slip a fan into her pocket.

'I know! I know! you're going to the hall to see "The Seven Castles"!' she cried, adding resolutely, 'and I *shall* go, for Mother said I might see it; and I've got my rag-money, and it was mean not to tell me in time.'

'Just listen to me a minute, and be a good child,' said Meg, soothingly. 'Mother doesn't wish you to go this week, because your eyes are not well enough yet to bear the light of this fairy piece. Next week you can go with Beth and Hannah, and have a nice time.'

'I don't like that half as well as going with you and Laurie. Please let me; I've been sick with this cold so long, and shut up, I'm dying for some fun. Do, Meg! I'll be ever so good,' pleaded Amy, looking as pathetic as she could.

'Suppose we take her. I don't believe Mother would mind, if we bundle her up well,' began Meg.

'If *she* goes *I* shan't; and if I don't, Laurie won't like it; and it will be very rude, after he invited only us, to go and drag in Amy. I should think she'd hate to poke herself where she isn't wanted,' said Jo, crossly, for she disliked the trouble of overseeing a fidgety child, when she wanted to enjoy herself.

Her tone and manner angered Amy, who began to put her boots on, saying, in her most aggravating way, 'I *shall* go; Meg says I may; and if I pay for myself, Laurie hasn't anything to do with it.'

'You can't sit with us, for our seats are reserved, and you mustn't sit alone; so Laurie will give you his place, and that will spoil our pleasure; or he'll get another seat for you, and that isn't proper, when you weren't asked. You shan't stir a step; so you may just stay where you are,' scolded Jo, crosser than ever, having just pricked her finger in her hurry.

Sitting on the floor, with one boot on, Amy began to cry, and Meg to reason with her, when Laurie called from below, and the two girls hurried down, leaving their sister wailing; for now and then she forgot her grown-up ways, and acted like a spoilt child. Just as the party were setting out, Amy called over the bannisters, in a threatening voice, 'You'll be sorry for this, Jo March; see if you ain't.'

'Fiddlesticks!' returned Jo, slamming the door.

They had a charming time, for 'The Seven Castles of the Diamond Lake' was as brilliant and wonderful as heart could wish. But, in spite of the comical red imps, sparkling elves, and gorgeous princes and princesses, Jo's pleasure had a drop of bitterness in it; the fairy queen's yellow curls reminded her of Amy; and between the acts she amused herself with wondering what her sister would do to make her 'sorry for it'. She and Amy had had many lively skirmishes in the course of their lives, for both had quick tempers, and were apt to be violent when fairly roused. Amy teased Jo, Jo irritated Amy, and semi-occasional explosions occurred, of which both were much ashamed afterwards. Although the oldest, Jo had the least self-control, and had hard times trying to curb the fiery spirit which was continually getting her into trouble; her anger never lasted long, and having humbly confessed her fault she sincerely repented and tried to do better. Her sisters used to say that they rather liked to get Jo into a fury because she was such an angel afterwards. Poor Jo tried desperately to be good, but her bosom enemy was always ready to flame up and defeat her; and it took years of patient effort to subdue it.

When they got home they found Amy reading in the parlour. She assumed an injured air as they came in; never lifted her eyes from her book, or asked a single question. Perhaps curiosity might have conquered resentment, if Beth had not been there to inquire, and receive a glowing description of the play. On going up to put away her best hat, Jo's first look was towards the bureau; for, in their last quarrel, Amy had soothed her feelings by turning Jo's top drawer upside-down on the floor. Everything was in its place, however, and after a hasty glance into her various closets, bags, and boxes, Jo decided that Amy had forgiven and forgotten her wrongs.

There Jo was mistaken; for next day she made a discovery which produced a tempest. Meg, Beth, and Amy were sitting together, late in the afternoon, when Jo burst into the room, looking excited, and demanding breathlessly, 'Has anyone taken my book?'

Meg and Beth said 'No', at once, and looked surprised; Amy poked the fire, and said nothing. Jo saw her colour rise, and was down upon her in a minute.

'Amy, you've got it.'

'No, I haven't.'

'You know where it is, then!'

'No, I don't.'

'That's a fib!' cried Jo, taking her by the shoulders and looking fierce enough to frighten a much braver child than Amy.

'It isn't. I haven't got it, don't know where it is now, and don't care.'

'You know something about it, and you'd better tell at once, or I'll make you,' and Jo gave her a slight shake.

'Scold as much as you like, you'll never see your silly old book again,' cried Amy, getting excited in her turn.

'Why not?'

'I burnt it up.'

'What! my little book I was so fond of, and worked over, and meant to finish before Father got home! Have you really burnt it?' said Jo, turning very pale, while her eyes kindled and her hands clutched Amy nervously.

'Yes, I did! I told you I'd make you pay for being so cross yesterday, and I have, so –'

Amy got no further, for Jo's hot temper mastered her, and she shook Amy till her teeth chattered in her head; crying in a passion of grief and anger:

'You wicked, wicked girl! I never can write it again and I'll never forgive you as long as I live.'

Meg flew to rescue Amy, and Beth to pacify Jo, but Jo was quite beside herself; and with a parting box on her sister's ear, she rushed out of the room up to the old sofa in the garret, and finished her fight alone.

The storm cleared up below, for Mrs March came home, and, having heard the story, soon brought Amy to a sense of the wrong she had done her sister. Jo's book was the pride of her heart, and was regarded by her family as a literary sprout of great promise. It was only half a dozen little fairy tales, but Jo had worked over them patiently, putting her whole heart into her work, hoping to make something good enough to print. She had just copied them with great care, and had destroyed the old manuscript, so that Amy's bonfire had consumed the loving work of several years. It seemed a small loss to others, but to Jo it was a dreadful calamity, and she felt that it never could be made up to her. Beth mourned as for a departed kitten, and Meg refused to defend her pet; Mrs March looked grave and grieved, and Amy felt that no one would love her till she had asked pardon for the act which she now regretted more than any of them.

When the tea-bell rang Jo appeared, looking so grim

and unapproachable, that it took all Amy's courage to say meekly:

'Please forgive me, Jo; I'm very, very sorry.'

'I never shall forgive you,' was Jo's stern answer; and from that moment she ignored Amy entirely.

No one spoke of the great trouble – not even Mrs March – for all had learned by experience that when Jo was in that mood words were wasted; and the wisest course was to wait till some little accident, or her own generous nature, softened Jo's resentment, and healed the breach. It was not a happy evening; for though they sewed as usual, while their mother read aloud from Bremer, Scott, or Edgeworth, something was wanting and the sweet home peace was disturbed. They felt this most when singing time came; for Beth could only play, Jo stood dumb as a stone, and Amy broke down, so Meg and Mother sang alone. But in spite of their efforts to be as cheery as larks, the flute-like voices did not seem to chord as well as usual, and all felt out of tune.

As Jo received her good-night kiss, Mrs March whispered gently: 'My dear, don't let the sun go down upon your anger; forgive each other, help each other, and begin again tomorrow.'

Jo wanted to lay her head down on that motherly bosom, and cry her grief and anger all away, but tears were an unmanly weakness, and she felt so deeply injured that she really *couldn't* quite forgive yet. So she winked hard, shook her head, and said gruffly, because Amy was listening: 'It was an abominable thing, and she don't deserve to be forgiven.'

With that she marched off to bed and there was no merry or confidential gossip that night.

Love Between Brothers and Sisters

Whatever brawls disturb the street,
   There should be peace at home;
Where sisters dwell and brothers meet,
   Quarrels should never come.

Birds in their little nests agree,
   And 'tis a shameful sight,
When children of one family,
   Fall out and chide and fight.

Isaac Watts (1674–1748)

ELEANOR GRAHAM

FROM The Children Who Lived in a Barn

Here's a sister who has to look after her family while
their parents are abroad – and has to convince an
interfering social worker that they can manage by
themselves even though they are desperately short of
money. This book was written by Eleanor Graham,
the first Editor of Puffin Books.

*   *   *

Sue was going over school clothes. Shoes, stockings, and
handkerchiefs worried her a good deal for she knew the
children must all look neat and tidy.

'School *is* going to be a bother,' she moaned to herself,
thinking of the time it would take out of her day and the
extra work involved in keeping up these most essential
appearances.

Baths over night, she decided too, so that the morning
wash might be easier.

'Woe betide anyone who leaves this house with grubby
knees or hands,' she remarked to the only other member of
the family who happened to be present and that was Alice
who only tossed her head. 'And no playing about on the
way to school either,' Sue went on not at all put out by
lack of an appreciative audience, 'you've all got to arrive at
school as clean as when you start out. And we shan't be
able to buy new clothes ever – so you'll all have to take
terrific care of what we've got.'

'Take care yourself,' returned Alice rudely.

'I'm worse off than you,' Sue replied seriously, 'I *could* make you a frock out of one of mine but if my clothes go, what *shall* I do?'

Alice giggled annoyingly.

'You are a little beast,' Sue told her comfortably, 'a real little pig. You don't care what happens, do you?'

'I wouldn't tell you if I did,' the little one returned triumphantly.

Sue gave it up. Sometimes she wondered whether Alice had always been so difficult, so thoroughly awkward. She had thought of her at home as rather a sweet little thing but of course Mother had made a lot of difference to each of them. She herself had been far better tempered with Mother to rely on for things and the twins never behaved so idiotically then as they did almost all the time now. 'Well, it's no good getting disheartened at this stage,' she told herself, turning away from Alice and examining the heels and toes of more socks.

She got up next morning when the alarm went off, lit the fire and put the kettle on, groaning to herself because water took so long to heat over a twig fire, and when she went to the wood bin she found it empty.

'Bob must do something about this wood business,' she declared vexedly. It was his job though the twins mainly fetched in the twigs and branches. There was still plenty of wood in the spinney, including a good tree trunk which the farmer had said they could chop up for themselves. And he had lent Bob a hatchet for that purpose. It was not too thick a tree for him to manage. He simply had not bothered. And now Sue had to go padding out in her dressing-gown and everything wet with dew. She *was* cross.

'That'll never burn,' she exclaimed as she flung a faggot

down beside the stove. 'Bob, you might see that there's plenty of wood in at night and some drying beside the fire ready for the morning.'

Bob rashly poked his head out of the blankets at the sound of her voice but very quickly tucked it in again when he heard her tone.

It was a particularly lovely morning though Sue had neither eyes nor ears for it. The sun was shining and the birds were singing ecstatically. She washed in the trough, keeping her back to the sun and determinedly looking on the dark side of everything. As soon as she was ready she called to the boys and Alice. Bob had worked up a considerable amount of indignation by then and had an answer ready for any complaint she might make. After all, had he not his hen-coops to see to before breakfast and wasn't it the twins' job to bring in wood anyway?

'Sam and Jum will have to cope with it,' he declared. 'I've other things to do and there's no reason either why young Alice shouldn't help. That kid never does a hand's turn for anyone.'

'Go on,' jeered Sue, 'while we work our fingers to the bone for her! I know!'

'I think you're a pig!' sobbed Alice, 'a pair of pigs!'

'Who cares what a little snippet like you thinks, anyway?' demanded Bob and he made a dash for the door before she had time to work up her answering howl to its full pitch.

'My goodness!' Sue muttered, shaking her head. She knew it was all her fault somehow, because she had wakened cross and had not been able to pull herself together since. The more she scolded, the worse everything became. She seized Alice, washed her, willy-nilly, dragged her into her knickers, skirt, and jersey. She was so energetic that Alice had no breath left to cry with but her fury against Sue and Bob did not lessen.

'I shall tell Miss Durden of you,' she said bitterly when she was free at last.

'Will you?' asked Sue, beginning to laugh, 'poor little sprat! It is a shame, isn't it? Bullied from morning to night!'

Alice looked obliquely at her, not quite sure what to make of this change of tone.

'I don't like you,' she said at last, 'you're mean to me.'

'I am, too,' Sue admitted cheerfully but quite unrepentant.

'Well then don't be,' screamed Alice. 'Mummy said you were to be nice to me.'

'She never did,' Sue replied, 'but I will for all that. Come here and help me make this wretched bed. Why on earth were we made girls, Al? Boys can always run off and do things outside, but we always have to tidy up indoors.'

At that moment the twins came in with a real load of wood between them and the news that Bob was on his way back to breakfast.

The farmer had slipped three eggs into Bob's pockets with a friendly nod and something indistinct about *school*, and Sue cheered at the sight of them though she remarked:

'Five into three won't go. At least, it's awkward. What shall we do with them? Hard boil and slice or scramble?'

'That fire won't make toast,' Bob remarked, frowning.

'All right. Let's keep them for tea. We've got porridge now and plenty of bread and dripping. We shall want comfort much more at the end of the day.'

As soon as breakfast was over Sue set the twins and Alice to clear the table while she swept the floor, and Bob attended to the hammocks. Then they all washed up, Sue doing the washing, the twins drying, and Alice carrying the clean dishes over to the dresser. When everything else was done, Sue rounded up the three and took a good look at them. Alice was still fairly clean. She only needed a sponge round her mouth and her hands washed, but Sambo and Jum might never have seen soap in their lives. Their knees were filthy and their nails appalling. Sue rubbed and scrubbed with loofah, pumice stone and brush, but had to give up in the end without reaching a very high standard of cleanliness.

'My shoes hurt,' Alice announced presently, standing awkwardly on one foot and holding out the other.

'So do mine,' shouted Jum. 'I'm going to take them off. Who wants to wear rotten old shoes?'

'*You're – not – to – take – them – off!*' Sue shouted in desperation. 'Stand quite still until I've got my hat and coat, then we shall have to run because it's getting frightfully late.'

At last they were off, each with hair smooth, cheeks rosy, brows shining and shoes and socks neat if not comfortable. Sue handed out handkerchiefs at the door with strict injunctions that each was to be returned to her when school for the day was over – and woe betide anyone who could not do so. Even Bob had a handkerchief doled out to him and was very huffy about it, though Sue reminded him that he was worse than anyone else about losing them.

'I don't lose them,' Bob said contrarily, 'and if I do, it's no more your business than mine.'

Sue took no notice of him, understanding better than Bob realized. The barn looked beautifully tidy as she closed the big doors and she turned the key in the padlock with a feeling of satisfaction that they had so far managed so well.

'You needn't think I'm going to walk to school, two by two in a blooming crocodile,' muttered Bob as they started up the path, and he doubled back and took the field path by himself.

'Well, well,' thought Sue, 'tempers are *not* so good this morning. I shall have to be more careful another time.'

Nevertheless she had to see that the children arrived at school clean and tidy so she made the boys walk in front while she held Alice's wrist for the child had doubled her hand up into an awkward fist and she struggled every step of the way, crying, '*Let me go! Let me go-ooooo, Sue!*' The twins intent on seeing the fun, walked backwards all the way giggling at Alice which made her worse.

'You are little beasts,' Sue told them all. 'You really are! Why can't any of you behave decently, just for once?'

So they arrived at school, hot and angry but in time and still clean.

Gloria, My Little Sister

Gloria, my little sister –
Well, I guess I would have missed her
If there hadn't ever been a
Gloria my little sister.

She's the one they all like better,
She's the one that gets the most.
When she stays up late they let her
Make a mess with cinnamon toast.
I get spanked if I just twist her
Arm, that little Gloria sister.
Still, I guess I would have missed her.

No one ever thinks she's tricky.
She spilled honey on the floor –
Mother found me very sticky.
Gloria was out the door.
When I caught her no one hit her.
I got spanked because I bit her
Ear, that little Gloria sister.
Still, I guess I would have missed her.

She can hardly throw a ball,
She can't ever catch at all.
Father said that I was mean
When my ball went through the screen
Door because she stepped aside.
Mother kissed her when she cried.
I was sorry that I missed her,
Gloria my little sister.

Brothers would have been all right.
Brothers help you in a fight,
Brothers put your worms on hooks,
Brothers lend you comic books.
Why can't fathers, why can't mothers
Give us large and useful brothers?
Still, I guess I would have missed her,
Gloria my little sister.

Russell Hoban

BETSY BYARS

FROM The Night Swimmers

Lots of the best stories happen when parents are not
there for various reasons. In Retta's case it's because
her mother has died and her father is working . . .

*   *   *

The Anderson kids entered their house noisily. They called
to each other. They snapped lights on and off as they
moved to their bedrooms. Roy paused in the living-room
and turned on the television, but as soon as Retta heard
The Tonight Show she came back and turned it off.

'Why not?' Roy whined.

'Because it's late. Now get to bed.' She pointed with one
hand to his bedroom. Her other hand was on her hip.
When she stood like that, like a real mother, Roy knew
there was no point in arguing.

'I never get to do anything!' he yelled. He stomped out
of the room.

There was no reason for them to be quiet because the
house was empty. Shorty Anderson, their father, was a
country-western singer who worked at night. Their mother
had been dead for two years, and Retta was raising the
three of them.

'Want me to get you something to eat?' Retta asked.
The success of the evening had made her feel more maternal
than usual.

In the hall the sound of Roy's stamping feet stopped. 'Peanut butter sandwich,' he said quickly.

'OK.'

'*With* bananas.'

'You want anything, Johnny?'

Johnny mumbled, 'No', sleepily. He was already in his pyjamas. He got into bed, rolled over, face to the wall, and fell asleep.

Beside him Roy was getting ready for his sandwich. He smoothed the sheet over his body as carefully as if it were a table-cloth. He wiped his hands, front and back, on his T-shirt. He loved to eat. The thought of the unexpected sandwich – Retta usually did not allow them to have bedtime snacks – made his face glow with pleasure.

'Kool-Aid too, please, Retta,' he called out in a polite voice.

In the kitchen, in the bright light over the sink, Retta was humming under her breath. She was slicing the banana, placing the slices in neat rows on the peanut butter. In the window she could see her reflection, her long wet hair swinging about her face. She smiled at herself.

Retta was happier tonight than she had been in months. She had been taking care of her brothers all her life, but this summer, since they had moved to this neighbourhood, it had become a lonely task. Tonight, however, they had had fun. She and her brothers were like friends now, she decided, doing things together. The summer vacation stretched ahead as one companionable, fun-filled day after another.

Retta finished making the sandwich, set it on top of a glass of milk, and carried it into her brother's bedroom. 'No Kool-Aid,' she said firmly as she handed the sandwich and milk to Roy.

'Thank you.' Roy was polite when it came to food. He

said 'please' and 'thank you' without even knowing he was saying the words. In kindergarten he never had to be reminded by Miss Elizabeth, 'Now, what do you say to Mrs Hartley for the cupcakes?' because he gasped out, 'Thank you', at the first glimpse of a white bakery box.

He turned his sandwich carefully, like a dog circling a bone. When he made his decision and took his first bite, an expression of contentment came over his face.

As usual, he began to eat the crust of the bread first. He nibbled around the sandwich, trying to be dainty. He believed that you got more if you ate daintily.

Retta leaned against the chest of drawers, watching him work his way around his sandwich. Just when he finished the last of the crust and was ready to sink his teeth into the peanut butter and banana, she said, 'But, tomorrow, Roy, I'm putting you on a diet.'

He was so startled that he almost dropped his sandwich. He looked at her. In the soft bread remained the horseshoe print of his teeth. 'What?'

'I'm putting you on a diet tomorrow.'

'Why?' It was a cry of pain. 'I'm not fat.'

'You have to wear Chubbies now. Before long you'll be in Huskies.'

'I won't!'

'We'll talk about it tomorrow.'

'I won't be in Huskies. I promise!'

'We'll talk about it in the morning,' Retta said in the mature voice she had acquired from TV mothers.

'I promise I promise I promise –' He went up on his knees in a beggar's position. 'I promise I promise I –'

'Will you shut up and lie still?' Johnny rose up on one elbow and gave Roy a look of disgust and anger. 'I'm trying to sleep!'

'Well, I'm not going on a diet no matter what!' To

emphasize his point he began to take huge bites of his sandwich, gnawing at the bread like an animal, poking stray bananas into his mouth with his finger. When his mouth was completely filled, a solid mass of banana, peanut butter, and bread, he folded his arms over his chest. He stared defiantly at Retta. He smacked. He chewed. He kept on working his jaws long after the sandwich had been eaten.

Then he sat, arms folded, staring at Retta. 'Drink your milk,' she said.

He drank it without pausing, eyes always on Retta.

'Now, good night,' she said.

'Good night, *L*oretta,' he called after her, wanting to hurt her and knowing how much she hated to be called by her full name. She alone resented that she had been named after a country singer. '*L*oretta *Lynn*!'

She turned. 'Good night, Roy *A cuff*!'

'*L*oretta Lynn!'

'Roy Acuff!'

'*Shut up*!' Johnny yelled. He sat up in bed and glowered at them both.

Brother

I had a little brother
And I brought him to my mother
And I said I want another
Little brother for a change.

But she said don't be a bother
So I took him to my father
And I said this little bother
Of a brother's very strange.

But he said one little brother
Is exactly like another
Misbehaves a bit, he said.

So I took my little brother
From my mother and my father
And I put the little bother
Of a brother back to bed.

Mary Ann Hoberman

The Quarrel

I quarrelled with my brother,
I don't know what about,
One thing led to another
And somehow we fell out.
The start of it was slight,
The end of it was strong,
He said he was right,
I knew he was wrong!
We hated one another.
The afternoon turned black.
Then suddenly my brother
Thumped me on the back,
And said, 'Oh, *come* along!
We can't go on all night –
I was in the wrong.'
So he was in the right.

Eleanor Farjeon

My Sister

My sister's remarkably light,
She can float to a fabulous height.
It's a troublesome thing,
But we tie her with string,
And we use her instead of a kite.

Margaret Mahy

RUMER GODDEN

Sisters In Exile

FROM A Time to Dance, No Time to Weep

Now for three pairs of sisters who *don't* quarrel. Rumer
Godden has written some marvellous books for
children, including the story of the Plantagenet family
who live in a doll's house. But this is a piece from her
own story, when she and her sister Jon were dumped
in a strange boarding school where they didn't understand the rules.

*   *   *

When Mam had driven away from the big red-brick build-
ing of St Monica's with its steepled church topped by a
cross, its playing fields and asphalt paths, we were taken by
a lay-sister to the nun in charge of the dormitories. 'These
are the two Goddens.' As Sister Irene looked down on us,
tall in her habit and wimple, graceful and cool, her eyes
amused, it was obvious that this was what she saw, two
odd little fishes out of water.

We must have looked odd. The school coats were thicker
than anything we had ever worn and we moved stiffly in
them like marionettes; their dark blue made us seem more
sallow than we were. We had not worn gloves before and
we held our fingers straight out in our new brown kid
gloves. 'Curl your fingers round,' said Sister Irene. 'Unbend
them.' Our noses and eyes were swollen and pink with
weeping and cold, and our pie-dish hats would not sit

down on our curly hair. 'That hair must be tied back!' said Sister Irene and, before she took us downstairs, she plaited it for us – it was to be one of our disgraces that we did not know how to plait. My hair soon adapted itself but Jon's obstinately curled in its plait; it was a real pigtail.

I still cannot fathom why, as it had been decided that Fa would go back to India alone and Mam would stay with us four in a rented house, we could not have been day girls which would have been more merciful; perhaps Fa and Mam had decided Jon was out of hand and, of course, where Jon went I went too. Perhaps our Grandmother prevailed – Mam was a chameleon in the way she took on other people's influences – and it was boarding school and not simply a boarding school, a High Anglican Convent.

In one week we collected more order marks than other girls in a term; we had order marks for answering back, for unpunctuality, for being untidy, and finally we were sent in to the Sister Superior, Sister Gertrude. 'You must learn that there is a place and time for everything and a way of doing everything,' said Sister Gertrude.

I have seen many headmistresses since then, some of them awe-inspiring, but I have never seen one as awful, in the old sense of the word, as Sister Gertrude. It is strange to think of a nun as arrogant and unkind but she was both. 'A time and a place for everything,' she said.

Jon looked at her with sincere and thoughtful eyes. 'But it takes time to learn the places,' said Jon.

Jon had more order marks than I, chiefly because she was more loyal to our upbringing, more honest. I found ways of avoiding trouble and I tried to help her but this was something that was not allowed. St Monica's was a convent school founded on religion; twice a day we went to chapel, three times a day the Angelus sounded through the school and we had prayers in the big gymnasium every day. Sister Gertrude read the lessons and the girls took it in turn to read the collect for the day – not, of course, either of us because of the chi-chi accent. 'Blessed are the meek,' read Sister Gertrude, or 'God has chosen the foolish things of the world to confound the wise.' 'God hath chosen the weak' . . . 'things which are despised hath God chosen.' A little feeble-minded girl, Florence, was very much despised; Sister Gertrude treated her with heart-rending coldness. 'The first shall be last,' read sister Gertrude, but the work and life of the school, its conduct and lessons and games, seemed founded on a precept that was quite opposite; there was a scramble to be first, to be best, to be successful, and it was shameful to be last, to be slow, to be weak.

By degrees we learnt that there was something that reconciled these extremes; it was called 'being sporting'.

'You and your sister really must learn to be sports,' said the mighty Games Captain to me. Probably no two girls ever went to school who were more feeble sports.

We were sneaks, as well; when Sister asked about an over-turned inkpot or a scribble on the blackboard, 'Who did this?' Jon and I answered obligingly, 'Greta Robinson' or 'Mary Smith'. How were we to know that Greta or Mary would be made to stand on the rostrum in the gymnasium in front of everybody or be sent to bed with the Juniors or have dry bread for tea? When, in India, Fa had asked, 'Who did this?' and we had said, 'Jon' or 'Rumer', nothing had ever happened.

All the same I achieved a certain popularity – for a while. The school went out, two by two, in a crocodile; for some reason sisters were not allowed to walk together and, as no one else ever chose Jon or me, we would wait, hanging about with the other rejects, until a nun paired us off; Jon was either made to walk with the nun or else a

Chinese girl, Ansie, with whom nobody wanted to walk because she spoke very little English. I usually had Florence who never spoke at all. I grew quite fond of Florence; I could tell her stories and, as she was silent, the stories were not interrupted; it was like writing aloud.

The girls in front or the girls behind must have listened to my stories as we moved along in our blue-coated, blue-hatted crocodile, for soon I was being asked to tell them in recreation, in the garden breaks, in sewing hour, especially stories about India. It was so intoxicating to be suddenly interesting that it went to my head and I told everything that the girls wanted to hear about India: about rajahs, elephants, howdahs, faithful brown servants, curries, tigers and snakes. It led to trouble: '. . . with his foot on the python, my father looked up,' I was saying, one day. 'He looked up and saw not one but three tigers.'

'That's not true,' said a girl with some sense.

'I swear it's true . . .' but there was Sister Irene and she beckoned me.

'Come with me,' said Sister Irene. Feeling small and chilled, I went.

The nuns used public opinion as a rod and I was publicly shamed. As a branded liar I was told to wear my class badge upside-down. 'All people are liars,' said Jon and wore hers upside-down too. When told she must not, she still did it and was sent to Sister Gertrude.

'This spirit must be broken,' Sister Gertrude told her and proud mature Jon was sent to bed with the Juniors.

ERICH KÄSTNER

FROM Lottie and Lisa

Lottie and Lisa are twins, but until they went to the
same holiday school they didn't know it, for Lisa lives
with their father and Lottie with their mother, and
they don't really understand why.

*   *   *

The two girls stuck together like burrs. Truddie, Steffie,
Monica, Christine, and the rest were sometimes cross with
Lisa and jealous of Lottie. What good did it do? None at
all! Where had they slipped off to now?

They had slipped off to the locker-room. Lottie took two
identical pinafores from her locker, gave one to her sister,
and tied the other round herself.

'Mummy bought these,' she said, 'at Pollinger's.'

'Aha,' exclaimed Lisa. 'That's the store in Neuhauser
Street, near – What is the name of that gate?'

'Carl's Gate.'

'That's right – near Carl's Gate.'

By now they were mutually well informed about each
other's way of life, school-friends, neighbours, teachers,
and flats. For Lisa everything connected with her mother
was terribly important. And Lottie longed to know
anything, any little thing, that her sister could tell her
about her father. For days on end they talked of nothing

else. And in bed at night they whispered together for hours. Each discovered a new and strange continent. What had been hitherto encompassed by their childhood's sky was, they suddenly realized, only half a world.

And at moments when they were not hard at work fitting together these two halves in order to get a glimpse of the whole, another subject excited them, another mystery tormented them: Why were their parents no longer together?

'First, of course, they got married,' explained Lisa for the hundredth time. 'Then they had us two. And they christened me Lisa and you Lottie because Mummy's name is Lisalotte. That's pretty, isn't it? They must have been fond of each other in those days, mustn't they?'

'I'm sure of it,' said Lottie. 'And then they must have quarrelled. And parted. And they bisected us in just the same way as they bisected Mummy's christian name.'

'They really ought to have asked us before they cut us in half.'

'But at that time we hadn't even learnt to speak.'

The two sisters smiled helplessly. Then they linked arms and went into the garden.

The post had come. Everywhere, in the grass, on the wall, and on the garden benches, little girls were sitting, reading letters.

Lottie held in her hands the photograph of a man of about thirty-five. She was looking with loving eyes at her father. So that was how he looked. And this was the sort of feeling you had round your heart when you had a real, live father!

Lisa read what he had written to her: 'My dearest, only child!' – 'What a liar!' she said, looking up. 'He knows perfectly well he has twins!' She went on reading: 'I think

you must have quite forgotten what your old father looks
like. Otherwise you wouldn't be so anxious to have a
photograph of him just before the end of the holidays.
First I thought I would send you a picture of me as a baby
– one that shows me lying naked on a polar-bear skin. But
you wrote that it must be an absolutely brand-new one. So
I rushed off to the photographer's, though I really couldn't
spare the time, and explained to him just why I needed it in
such a hurry . . . I told him that unless he took my picture
my Lisa wouldn't recognize me when I went to the station
to meet her. By good luck he saw how important it was.
And so you're getting it in good time. I'm sorry for the
young lady supervisors at your holiday home. I hope you
don't lead them such a dance as you do your father – who
sends you a thousand greetings and is longing to have you
home again.'

'Lovely!' said Lottie. 'And funny! And yet on the picture he looks quite serious.'

'He was probably too shy to laugh in front of the photographer,' speculated Lisa. 'He always looks serious in front of other people. But when we're alone he can be quite jolly.'

Lottie held the photograph tight. 'Can I really keep it?'

'Of course,' said Lisa. 'That's why I got him to send it.'

GEORGE MAYHEW

A Victorian Flower-Girl

FROM London Labour and the London Poor

This eleven-year-old child sold flowers in the street along with her sister, aged fifteen; her brother, thirteen, was a costermonger's boy.

*   *   *

They lived in one of the streets near Drury Lane. The room was large, and one dim candle lit it; the walls were bare and damp; the furniture consisted of a crazy table and a few chairs, and in the centre of the room an old fourposter bed was shared by the two sisters and their brother.

[The flower-girl's words:]

'I sell flowers, sir; we live almost on flowers when they are to be got ... It's no use offering anything that's not sweet. I sell primroses, when they are in, and violets, and wall-flowers, and stocks, and roses of different sorts, and pinks, and carnations, and lilies of the valley, and lavender and moss-roses. Gentlemen are our best customers. I've heard that they buy flowers to give to the ladies.

'My father was tradesman in Ireland, but I was born in London. None of us ever saw our father. Mother was charwoman; she died seven years ago last Guy Fawkes day. We've earned our own bread ever since and never had any help but from the neighbours.

'I buy my flowers at Covent Garden. I pay a shilling for a dozen bunches, whatever flowers are in. Out of every two bunches I can make three, at 1d [one penny) each. We make the bunches up ourselves; we get the rush to tie them with for nothing. The paper for a dozen costs a penny; sometimes only a halfpenny. The two of us doesn't make less than 6d [six pence] a day, unless it's very ill luck. We do better on oranges in March and April than on flowers – oranges keep better you see, sir. We make a shilling a day on oranges, the two of us.

'I always keep 1 shilling stock-money if I can. If it's bad weather, so bad we can't sell flowers at all, and so if we've had to spend our stock-money on a bit of bread, the landlady lends us 1s [one shilling] . . . if she has one, or she borrows it off a neighbour if she hasn't.

'We live on bread and tea, and sometimes a fresh herring of a night. Sometimes we don't eat a bite all day when we're out, sometimes we take a bit of bread with us, or buy a bit.'

The landlady said that these two girls were never out of doors all the time she had known them after six at night.

An Accident Happened to My Brother Jim

An accident happened to my brother Jim
When somebody threw a tomato at him –
Tomatoes are juicy and don't hurt the skin,
But this one was specially packed in a tin.

Anon

LEWIS CARROLL

A Letter to Two Sisters

Here's a letter from Lewis Carroll to two of his seven sisters while he was away at boarding school. Much later on, when he was grown up, he wrote *Alice in Wonderland*.

*   *   *

My dear Fanny and Memy,

I hope you are getting on well, as also the sweet twins. The boys I think that I like the best, are Harry Austin, and all the Tates of which there are 7 besides a little girl who came down to dinner the first day, but not since, and I also like Edmund Tremlet, and William and Edward Swire. Tremlet is a sharp little fellow about 7 years old, the youngest in the school. I also like Kemp and Mawley. The rest of the boys that I know are Bertram, Harry and Dick Wilson, and two Robinsons, I will tell you all about them when I return. The boys have played two tricks upon me which were these – they first proposed to play at 'King of the Cobblers' and asked if I would be king to which I agreed. Then they made me sit down and sat (on the ground) in a circle round me, and told me to say 'Go to work' which I said, and they immediately began kicking me and knocking me on all sides. The next game they proposed was 'Peter, the red lion', and they made a mark on a tombstone (for we were playing in the churchyard)

190

and one of the boys walked with his eyes shut, holding out his finger, trying to touch the mark; then a little boy came forward to lead the rest and led a good many very near the mark; at last it was my turn; they told me to shut my eyes well, and the next minute I had my finger in the mouth of one of the boys, who stood (I believe) before the tombstone with his mouth open. For 2 nights I slept alone, and for the rest of the time with Ned Swire. The boys play me no tricks now.

The only fault (tell Mama) that there has been was coming in one day to dinner just after grace. On Sunday we went to church in the morning, and sat in a large pew with Mr Fielding, the church we went to is close by Mr Tate's house, we did not go in the afternoon but Mr Tate read a discourse to the boys on the 5th commandment. We went to church again in the evening. Papa wished me to tell him all the texts I had heard preached upon, please to tell him that I could not hear it in the morning nor hardly one sentence of the sermon, but the one in the evening was 1 Cor.1.23. I believe it was a farewell sermon, but I am not sure. Mrs Tate has looked through my clothes and left in the trunk a great many that will not be wanted. I have had 3 misfortunes in my clothes etc. 1st I cannot find my tooth-brush, so that I have not brushed my teeth for 3 or 4 days, 2nd I cannot find my blotting paper, and 3rd I have no shoe-horn. The chief games are, football, wrestling, leap frog, and fighting. Excuse bad writing.

Yr affect. brother CHARLES.

GRANDPARENTS

Grandparents can be the most useful members of any family that is lucky enough to have them in good health (and living near by!). Apart from being reliable baby-sitters, they have wonderfully long memories, and are good to write poems about. And some can also be surprising – like Super Gran – who is accidentally struck by a magic ray and at once joins the local football team!

FORREST WILSON

FROM Super Gran

Granny Smith, an ordinary, little, old white-haired lady, resting on a seat in the public park, began to feel decidedly peculiar . . .

Granny Smith was old and her eyesight and hearing were not as good as they used to be; she needed glasses with extra-thick lenses, and she needed a hearing-aid.

Her poor, thin old body was stiff and full of rheumatism, and her legs were weak; she needed a walking-stick to help her get along. She felt the cold so much, even in summer, that she had to wrap up well; so she was wearing a thick coat, a scarf and a tartan tammy.

Her arms were so frail that she couldn't carry even the lightest shopping-bag, so she used a shopping-trolley. And she *so* hated being seen with it – she said it made her look old!

So here she sat, resting on a park bench because she could walk only a few hundred yards at a time, without getting completely tired out. Her grandson, freckle-faced Willard, whom she called Willie, for short, had accompanied her to the park, but he'd left her to rest while he played football with some of his pals, a few yards away. Willard wore, as he always did, a football shirt in the red-and-white stripes of his local League team.

Suddenly . . . a beam of blue light shot out of nowhere,

it seemed, and struck the little old lady. It engulfed her and the seat, for about a minute, and then it faded and disappeared, as suddenly as it had appeared.

And it was then that Granny Smith began to feel peculiar. And it was that one minute which changed her life completely. For that was the start of SUPER GRAN . . .

It was also just about then that the girl, Edison Faraday Black, appeared on the scene. She came rushing down a grassy slope towards Granny Smith, shouted something excitedly . . . and then tripped, as she always seemed to do, fell and rolled headlong down the slope, ending up at Granny Smith's feet.

The auburn-haired girl stood up and dusted herself down. 'Are you all right, lady?' she asked, concerned. 'I saw the ray hit you and . . .'

Granny Smith, feeling *most* peculiar by now, put her hand to her head. 'Aye . . . I . . . I think so, lassie . . .'

The little old lady wasn't really sure. What *was* happening, she wondered. For something definitely *was* happening to her. Something strange. She could feel it in her bones; she could feel it all through her thin, frail body.

'It was that rotter, the Inventor, I *know* it was, it must have been,' Edison said, as she looked all around, towards the dozen or so large houses near by which backed on to the public park. 'I know he lives round about here *some*where.' She frowned. 'And I've *al*most caught up with him. I just wish I knew which house was his.' She looked determined. 'But I'll *find* him, don't worry!'

Granny Smith couldn't take all this nonsense in. Not right then. She felt faint. Then, suddenly, she felt the opposite – 'un-faint' – whatever *that* meant, she thought.

She felt terrible, and then, suddenly, she felt great! It

was all very mysterious, and confusing. So she was too concerned with all these mixed feelings to be bothered listening to the girl's ramblings – or her 'bletherings' as she, Granny Smith, would have called them.

Her eyes, her ears, her bones, joints, limbs all seemed to be 'popping'. It was decidedly queer. It wasn't so much 'pains' she was having, it was 'sniap', she thought.

'"Sniap"? What's "sniap"?' she wondered, out loud.

'Pardon?' Edison frowned.

Granny Smith giggled. '"Sniap" is "pains" backwards! The *opposite* of "pains",' she explained to the girl. 'I'm having lots of lovely "sniap"!' She had just invented the word and was extremely proud of her cleverness. She could never have thought of anything like that before this happened.

She had a kind of mist in front of her eyes, so she pulled her glasses off – and found she could see perfectly! She threw them away and they landed on the nose of a little white poodle, sniffing around some bushes ... FIFTY YARDS AWAY.

She listened. She could hear the boys' shouts deafeningly loud; she could hear the sparrows in the distant tree-tops, chirping as if they were sitting on her shoulder! So she pulled her hearing-aid off and tossed it away, too. And it hit the little, be-spectacled poodle on the head!

Granny Smith stood up, smiled – and bent down to touch her toes; something she hadn't been able to do for about thirty years!

'Are ... are you *sure* you're all right?' Edison asked, frowning. 'Oh! Careful! What're you doing?' She moved towards Granny Smith to steady, or catch her, if she fell.

But the little old lady didn't need her help. 'I'm ... I'm not sure, lassie,' she said, as she straightened up. Then she grinned, hugely. 'Aye ... aye ... I *am* sure. I *am* all right.

197

I'm *more* than all right. I'm terrific! Yippee!'

She yelled with delight, did a little jig, kicked her heels together, threw her tartan tammy into the air, jumped about . . . and threw her walking-stick away! 'I won't be needing *that* thing again!'

The little white poodle, glasses on its nose and the hearing-aid strung over its back, saw the stick flying towards it . . . and ran for its life!

Things were happening too quickly for Edison, however. Only a few minutes ago she'd been hovering at the top of the grassy slope, near the park railings, when she'd seen Granny Smith walking slowly and painfully along, leaning on her walking-stick and clutching at the arm of her grandson, who had been trailing the shopping-trolley along. And now, after only one little shot from the machine's ray, Edison was looking at a miracle! 'So it *does* work on people!' she murmured to herself.

She felt a surge of pride in her father, at the thought of his machine working; it definitely *was* a Super-machine! But then she had another surge – of anger, for the hated Inventor, who had stolen it from him.

Edison came out of her daydream when she realized that Granny Smith was looking towards the boys, and was saying: 'I'm away to have a game of football, lassie! Are you coming?' Her eyes gleamed.

'Oh no!' the girl gasped. 'Maybe you're not . . . uh . . . I mean, maybe you're not strong enough yet for that, and besides . . .'

'Blethers!' The old lady took off her heavy winter coat and threw it over the bench; and the scarf followed. Then she put her tartan tammy on at a jaunty angle, as she ran to join the boys. 'Of *course* I'm strong enough for a silly wee game of football. Who says I'm not! What d'you think I am . . . a little old lady?'

'But you *are* a little old la . . .!' The girl shrugged. What was the use?

Edison picked up the coat and scarf, took the handle of the trolley, and started to trot after the old lady. She knew she would never catch up with her, for Granny Smith was now giving a good imitation of an Olympic sprinter, as she sped towards the boys.

Babbling and Gabbling

My Granny's an absolute corker,
My Granny's an absolute cracker,
But she's Britain's speediest talker
and champion yackety-yacker!

Everyone's fond of my Granny,
Everyone thinks she's nice,
But before you can say Jack Robinson,
My Granny's said it twice!

Kit Wright

TOVE JANSSON

The Morning Swim
FROM The Summer Book

Perhaps you can get the best out of grandmothers when
you have them all to yourself. Certainly Sophia thought
so in this story from *The Summer Book*.

*   *   *

It was an early, very warm morning in July, and it had
rained during the night. The bare granite steamed, the
moss and crevices were drenched with moisture, and all the
colours everywhere had deepened. Below the veranda, the
vegetation in the morning shade was like a rain forest of
lush, evil leaves and flowers, which she had to be careful
not to break as she searched. She held one hand in front of
her mouth and was constantly afraid of losing her balance.

'What are you doing?' asked little Sophia.

'Nothing,' her grandmother answered. 'That is to say,'
she added angrily, 'I'm looking for my false teeth.'

The child came down from the veranda. 'Where did you
lose them?' she asked.

'Here,' said her grandmother. 'I was standing right there
and they fell somewhere in the peonies.' They looked
together.

'Let me,' Sophia said. 'You can hardly walk. Move
over.'

She dived beneath the flowering roof of the garden and
crept among green stalks and stems. It was pretty and

mysterious down on the soft black earth. And there were the teeth, white and pink, a whole mouthful of old teeth. 'I've got them!' the child cried, and stood up. 'Put them in.'

'But you can't watch,' Grandmother said. 'That's private.'

Sophia held the teeth behind her back.

'I want to watch,' she said.

So Grandmother put the teeth in, with a smacking noise. They went in very easily. It had really hardly been worth mentioning.

'When are you going to die?' the child asked.

And Grandmother answered, 'Soon. But that is not the least concern of yours.'

'Why?' her grandchild asked.

She didn't answer. She walked out on the rock and on toward the ravine.

'We're not allowed out there!' Sophia screamed.

'I know,' the old woman answered disdainfully. 'Your father won't let either one of us go out to the ravine, but we're going anyway, because your father is asleep and he won't know.'

They walked across the granite. The moss was slippery. The sun had come up a good way now, and everything was steaming. The whole island was covered with a bright haze. It was very pretty.

'Will they dig a hole?' asked the child amiably.

'Yes,' she said. 'A big hole.' And she added, insidiously, 'Big enough for all of us.'

'How come?' the child asked.

They walked on toward the point.

'I've never been this far before,' Sophia said. 'Have you?'

'No,' her grandmother said.

They walked all the way out on to the little promontory, where the rock descended into the water in terraces that became fainter and fainter until there was total darkness. Each step down was edged with a light green seaweed fringe that swayed back and forth with the movement of the sea.

'I want to go swimming,' the child said. She waited for opposition, but none came. So she took off her clothes, slowly and nervously. She glanced at her grandmother – you can't depend on people who just let things happen. She put her legs in the water.

'It's cold,' she said.

'Of course it's cold,' the old woman said, her thoughts somewhere else. 'What did you expect?'

The child slid in up to her waist and waited anxiously.

'Swim,' her grandmother said. 'You can swim.'

It's deep, Sophia thought. She forgets I've never swum in deep water unless somebody was with me. And she climbed out again and sat down on the rock.

'It's going to be a nice day today,' she declared.

The sun had climbed higher. The whole island, and the sea, were glistening. The air seemed very light.

'I can dive,' Sophia said. 'Do you know what it feels like when you dive?'

'Of course I do,' her grandmother said. 'You let go of everything and get ready and just dive. You can feel the seaweed against your legs. It's brown, and the water's clear, lighter toward the top, with lots of bubbles. And you glide. You hold your breath and glide and turn and come up, let yourself rise and breathe out. And then you float. Just float.'

'And all the time with your eyes open,' Sophia said.

'Naturally. People don't dive with their eyes shut.'

'Do you believe I can dive without me showing you?' the child asked.

'Yes, of course,' Grandmother said. 'Now get dressed. We can get back before he wakes up.'

The first weariness came closer. When we get home, she thought, when we get back I think I'll take a little nap. And I must remember to tell him this child is still afraid of deep water.

Granny Granny Please Comb My Hair

Granny Granny please comb
my hair
you always take your time
you always take such care

You put me on a cushion
between your knees
you rub a little coconut oil
parting gentle as a breeze.

Mummy Mummy
she's always in a hurry-hurry
rush
she pulls my hair
sometimes she tugs

But Granny
you have all the time
in the world
and when you're finished
you always turn my head and say
'Now who's a nice girl'

Grace Nichols

LUCY M. BOSTON

FROM The Children of Green Knowe

Now for two special grandparents. Mrs Oldknow is Tolly's great grandmother. She lives alone in a strange and beautiful house, full of memories and sometimes ghostly children. At first Tolly thought she might be a witch, but she just had a special kind of magic. There are seven more *Green Knowe* books to read after this one.

*   *   *

It was a brilliant, sunny morning, and all the view was sparkling blue water, right away to the low hills in the distance. From this high window he could see where the course of the river should be, because of the pollard willows sticking out along each side of the bank, and because there the water was whirlpooled and creased and very brown and swift, while all the miles of overflow were just like blue silk.

'It really is like being in the Ark,' said Tolly.

'Yes, all the children used to call it the Ark. Your grandfather did, and he learnt it from his father, who learnt it from his, and so on right away back. But you called it that by yourself.'

Tolly sat in his pyjamas on the rocking-horse, making it go creak-croak, creak-croak.

'Do you know,' he said, 'when I was lying in bed with

my eyes shut I could hear the horse go creak-croak just like this? But when I opened my eyes it was quite still.'

'And did the mouse squeak under your pillow, and did the china dogs bark?'

'No,' said Tolly. 'Do they?'

Mrs Oldknow laughed. 'You seem ready for anything, that's something,' she said. 'Now get dressed and come down to breakfast.'

Tolly found his own way down the winding staircase, through the Music Room that was like a knight's hall, down the winding stairs again and across the entrance hall with its polished wooden children and queer sticks of flowers, and into the room where he had first met his great-grandmother the night before.

Breakfast was on the table, but she was standing by an open door throwing crumbs on to the doorstep for the birds. There were so many of them that they seemed to drop from the branches of the trees like ripe chestnuts when the tree is shaken, and as many were going up again with a piece of bread in their beaks as were coming down to get it. A few yards beyond the doorstep the garden was under water.

'The birds are very hungry. You see, they can't get worms, or seed, or ants' eggs until the floods go. Would you like to be introduced to them?'

'Yes please,' said Tolly.

'Come here, then,' said Mrs Oldknow; and although her back was rather bent and her face was wrinkled, when she looked at him so mischievously he could almost imagine she was a boy to play with. 'They love margarine better than anything,' she said. 'Hold out your hands.'

She spread his fingers and palms with margarine carefully all over, even between the fingers, then told him to go to the door and stand still, holding out both hands with the fingers open. She stood beside him and whistled. In a minute tits and robins and chaffinches and hedge-sparrows were fluttering round him till at last one ventured to perch on his thumb. After that the others were soon jostling to find room on his hands, fixing him with their bright eyes and opening their wings and cocking their tails to keep their balance. They pecked at the margarine on his palm and between his fingers. They tickled dreadfully, and Tolly wriggled and squealed so that they all flew away, but in a minute they were back.

'You must keep still and be quiet,' said Mrs Oldknow, laughing at him.

Tolly tried hard to obey her, but their beaks and little wiry clutching hands felt so queer that he had to shut his eyes and screw up his face to keep still. The tits hung on underneath and tickled in unexpected places.

While he was standing there pulling faces he heard a laugh so like a boy's that he could not believe his great-grandmother had made it, and opened his eyes to see who was there. There was no one else. Mrs Oldknow's eyes were fixed on his. The blackbirds were scolding in the branches because they were afraid to come on to his hands and could see the margarine was nearly finished. Then with a squabbling noise, like a crowd of rude people off a football bus, a flock of starlings arrived, snatching and pushing and behaving badly in every way.

'That will do,' said Mrs Oldknow. 'Starlings don't wait to be introduced to anybody. I'll give them some bread, and you can wipe your hands on these crusts and throw them to the blackbirds. Then run and wash your hands.'

She shut the door and sat down to breakfast. Tolly came quickly and sat down where a place was laid for him opposite the fireplace.

GEORGE MACDONALD

FROM The Princess and the Goblin

Princess Irene's great-great-grandmother appears and
disappears only when she is needed in a crisis. She
lives at the top of a winding staircase in a gloomy
castle, and is very important both to the Princess and
her friend Curdie.

*   *   *

When Irene came to the top, she found herself in a little
square place, with three doors, two opposite each other,
and one opposite the top of the stair. She stood for a
moment, without an idea in her little head what to do next.
But as she stood, she began to hear a curious humming
sound. Could it be the rain? No. It was much more gentle,
and even monotonous than the sound of the rain, which
now she scarcely heard. The low sweet humming sound
went on, sometimes stopping for a little while and then
beginning again. It was more like the hum of a very happy
bee that had found a rich well of honey in some globular
flower, than anything else I can think of at this moment.
Where could it come from? She laid her ear first to one of
the doors to hearken if it was there – then to another.
When she laid her ear against the third door, there could
be no doubt where it came from: it must be from something
in that room. What could it be? She was rather afraid, but
her curiosity was stronger than her fear, and she opened

the door very gently and peeped in. What do you think she saw? A very old lady who sat spinning.

Perhaps you will wonder how the princess could tell that the old lady was an old lady, when I inform you that not only was she beautiful, but her skin was smooth and white. I will tell you more. Her hair was combed back from her forehead and face, and hung loose far down and all over her back. That is not much like an old lady – is it? Ah! but it was white almost as snow. And although her face was so smooth, her eyes looked so wise that you could not have helped seeing she must be old. The princess, though she could not have told you why, did think her very old indeed – quite fifty, she said to herself. But she was rather older than that, as you shall hear.

While the princess stared bewildered, with her head just inside the door, the old lady lifted hers, and said, in a sweet, but old and rather shaky voice, which mingled very pleasantly with the continued hum of her wheel: 'Come in, my dear; come in. I am glad to see you.'

That the princess was a real princess you might see now quite plainly; for she didn't hang on to the handle of the door, and stare without moving, as I have known some do who ought to have been princesses but were only rather vulgar little girls. She did as she was told, stepped inside the door at once, and shut it gently behind her.

'Come to me, my dear,' said the old lady.

And again the princess did as she was told. She approached the old lady – rather slowly, I confess, but did not stop until she stood by her side, and looked up in her face with her blue eyes and the two melted stars in them.

'Why, what have you been doing with your eyes, child?' asked the old lady.

'Crying,' answered the princess.

'Why, child?'

'Because I couldn't find my way down again.'

'But you could find your way up.'

'Not at first – not for a long time.'

'But your face is streaked like the back of a zebra. Hadn't you a handkerchief to wipe your eyes with?'

'No.'

'Then why didn't you come to me to wipe them for you?'

'Please, I didn't know you were here. I will next time.'

'There's a good child!' said the old lady.

Then she stopped her wheel, and rose, and, going out of the room, returned with a little silver basin and a soft white towel, with which she washed and wiped the bright little face. And the princess thought her hands were so smooth and nice!

When she carried away the basin and towel, the little princess wondered to see how straight and tall she was, for, although she was so old, she didn't stoop a bit. She was dressed in black velvet with thick white heavy-looking lace about it; and on the black dress her hair shone like silver. There was hardly any more furniture in the room than there might have been in that of the poorest old woman who made her bread by her spinning. There was no carpet on the floor – no table anywhere – nothing but the spinning-wheel and the chair beside it. When she came back, she sat down again, and without a word began her spinning once more, while Irene, who had never seen a spinning-wheel, stood by her side and looked on. When the old lady had got her thread fairly going again, she said to the princess, but without looking at her:

'Do you know my name, child?'

'No, I don't know it,' answered the princess.

'My name is Irene.'

'That's *my* name!' cried the princess.

'I know that. I let you have mine. I haven't got your name. You've got mine.'

'How can that be?' asked the princess, bewildered. 'I've always had my name.'

'Your papa, the king, asked me if I had any objection to your having it; and, of course, I hadn't. I let you have it with pleasure.'

'It was very kind of you to give me your name – and such a pretty one,' said the princess.

'Oh, not so *very* kind!' said the old lady. 'A name is one of those things one can give away and keep all the same. I have a good many such things. Wouldn't you like to know who I am, child?'

'Yes, that I should – very much.'

'I'm your great-great-grandmother,' said the lady.

'What's that?' asked the princess.

'I'm your father's mother's father's mother.'

'Oh, dear! I can't understand that,' said the princess.

'I dare say not. I didn't expect you would. But that's no reason why I shouldn't say it.'

'Oh, no!' answered the princess.

'I will explain it all to you when you are older,' the lady went on. 'But you will be able to understand this much now: I came here to take care of you.'

Grandmother's Visit

This morning I was bad,
But it really didn't matter:
I came down the stairs
With a terrible clatter;
I jumped and I shouted,
I tried to pinch sister,
I called father 'Pop'
and the garbage man 'Mister';
I pretended I was deaf
And I said I liked beer.
But it really won't matter
'Cause Grandmother's here.

When Grandmother's here,
Then everything's fine:
She says a boy shouts
To strengthen his spine;
She says a boy jumps
To make him grow tall;
And when I pretend
She doesn't mind at all.
This morning I was bad,
But there's nothing to fear;
My troubles are over
When Grandmother's here!

Jonathan Blake

FRANCES HODGSON BURNETT

FROM Little Lord Fauntleroy

Some grandfathers can be quite hard to get on with, and the way Little Lord Fauntleroy managed to soften the heart of his fierce grandfather is as good as a fairy tale.

* * *

Cedric crossed the threshold into the room. It was a very large and splendid room, with massive carven furniture in it, and shelves upon shelves of books; the furniture was so dark, and the draperies so heavy, the diamond-paned windows were so deep, and it seemed such a distance from one end of it to the other, that, since the sun had gone down, the effect of it all was rather gloomy. For a moment Cedric thought there was nobody in the room, but soon he saw that by the fire burning on the wide hearth there was a large easy chair, and that in that chair someone was sitting – someone who did not at first turn to look at him.

But he had attracted attention in one quarter at least. On the floor, by the armchair, lay a dog, a huge tawny mastiff with body and limbs almost as big as a lion's; and this great creature rose majestically and slowly, and marched towards the little fellow with a heavy step.

Then the person in the chair spoke. 'Dougal,' he called, 'come back, sir.'

But there was no more fear in little Lord Fauntleroy's

214

heart than there was unkindness – he had been a brave little fellow all his life. He put his hand on the big dog's collar in the most natural way in the world, and they strayed forward together, Dougal sniffing as he went.

And then the Earl looked up. What Cedric saw was a large old man with shaggy white hair and eyebrows, and a nose like an eagle's beak between his deep fierce eyes. What the Earl saw was a graceful childish figure in a black velvet suit, with a lace collar, and with love-locks waving about the handsome, manly little face, whose eyes met his with a look of innocent good-fellowship. If the Castle was like the palace in a fairy story, it must be owned that little Lord Fauntleroy was himself rather like a small copy of the fairy prince, though he was not at all aware of the fact, and perhaps was rather a sturdy young model of a fairy. But there was a sudden glow of triumph and exultation in the fiery old Earl's heart as he saw what a strong beautiful boy this grandson was, and how unhesitatingly he looked up as he stood with his hand on the big dog's neck. It pleased the grim old nobleman that the child should show no shyness or fear, either of the dog or of himself.

Cedric looked at him just as he had looked at the woman at the lodge and at the housekeeper, and came quite close to him.

'Are you the Earl?' he said. 'I'm your grandson, you know, that Mr Havisham brought. I'm Lord Fauntleroy.'

He held out his hand because he thought it must be the polite and proper thing to do even with earls. 'I hope you are very well,' he continued, with the utmost friendliness. 'I'm very glad to see you.'

The Earl shook hands with him, with a curious gleam in his eyes; just at first he was so astonished that he scarcely knew what to say. He stared at the picturesque little apparition from under his shaggy brows, and took it all in from head to foot.

'Glad to see me, are you?' he said.

'Yes,' answered Lord Fauntleroy, 'very.'

There was a chair near him, and he sat down on it; it was a high-backed, rather tall chair, and his feet did not touch the floor when he had settled himself in it, but he seemed to be quite comfortable as he sat there and regarded his august relative intently and modestly.

'I've kept wondering what you would look like,' he remarked. 'I used to lie in my berth in the ship and wonder if you would be anything like my father.'

'Am I?' asked the Earl.

'Well,' Cedric replied, 'I was very young when he died, and I may not remember exactly how he looked, but I don't think you are like him.'

'You are disappointed, I suppose?' suggested his grand-father.

'Oh no!' responded Cedric politely. 'Of course you would like anyone to look like your father; but of course you would enjoy the way your grandfather looked, even if he wasn't like your father. You know how it is yourself about admiring your relations.'

The Earl leaned back in his chair and stared. He could not be said to know how it was about admiring his relations. He had employed most of his noble leisure in quarrelling violently with them, in turning them out of his house, and applying abusive epithets to them; and they all hated him cordially.

'Any boy would love his grandfather,' continued Lord Fauntleroy, 'especially one that had been as kind to him as you have been.'

Another queer gleam came into the old nobleman's eyes.

'Oh,' he said, 'I have been kind to you, have I?'

'Yes,' answered Lord Fauntleroy brightly; 'I'm ever so

much obliged to you about Bridget and the apple-woman and Dick!'

'Bridget!' exclaimed the Earl. 'Dick! The apple-woman!'

'Yes,' explained Cedric; 'the ones you gave me all that money for – the money you told Mr Havisham to give me if I wanted it.'

'Ha!' ejaculated his lordship. 'That's it, is it! The money you were to spend as you liked. What did you buy with it? I should like to hear something about that.'

He drew his shaggy eyebrows together and looked at the child sharply. He was secretly curious to know in what way the lad had indulged himself.

'Oh,' said Lord Fauntleroy, 'perhaps you didn't know about Dick and the apple-woman and Bridget. I forgot you lived such a long way off from them. They were particular friends of mine. And you see Michael had the fever –'

'Who's Michael?' asked the Earl.

'Michael is Bridget's husband, and they were in great trouble. When a man is sick and can't work and has twelve children you know how it is. And Michael had always been a sober man. And Bridget used to come to our house and cry. And the evening Mr Havisham was there, she was in the kitchen crying because they had almost nothing to eat and couldn't pay the rent; and I went in to see her, and Mr Havisham sent for me and he said you had given him some money for me. And I ran as fast as I could into the kitchen and gave it to Bridget; and that made it all right; and Bridget could scarcely believe her eyes. That's why I'm so obliged to you.'

'Oh,' said the Earl in his deep voice, 'that was one of the things you did for yourself, was it? What else?'

Dougal had been sitting by the tall chair; the great dog had taken its place there when Cedric sat down. Several times it had turned and looked up at the boy as if interested in the conversation. Dougal was a solemn dog, who seemed to feel altogether too big to take life's responsibilities lightly. The old Earl, who knew the dog well, had watched it with secret interest. Dougal was not a dog whose habit it was to make acquaintances rashly, and the Earl wondered somewhat to see how quietly the brute sat under the touch of the childish hand. And, just at this moment, the big dog gave little Lord Fauntleroy one more look of dignified scrutiny, and deliberately laid its huge, lion-like head on the boy's black-velvet knee.

The small hand went on stroking this new friend as Cedric answered:

'Well, there was Dick,' he said. 'You'd like Dick, he's so square.'

This was an Americanism the Earl was not prepared for.

'What does that mean?' he inquired.

Lord Fauntleroy paused a moment to reflect. He was not very sure himself what it meant. He had taken it for granted as meaning something very creditable because Dick had been fond of using it.

'I think it means that he wouldn't cheat anyone,' he exclaimed, 'or hit a boy who was under his size, and that he blacks people's boots very well and makes them shine as much as he can. He's a professional boot-black.'

'And he's one of your acquaintances, is he?' said the Earl.

'He's an old friend of mine,' replied his grandson. 'Not quite as old as Mr Hobbs, but quite old. He gave me a present before the ship sailed.'

He put his hand into his pocket and drew forth a neatly folded red object and opened it with an air of affectionate pride. It was the red silk handkerchief with the large purple horseshoes and heads on it.

'He gave me this,' said his young lordship. 'I shall keep

it always. You can wear it round your neck or keep it in your pocket. He bought it with the first money he earned after I bought Jake out and gave him the new brushes. It's a keepsake. I put some poetry in Mr Hobbs's watch. It was, "When this you see, remember me." When this I see I shall always remember Dick.'

The sensations of the Right Honourable the Earl of Dorincourt could scarcely be described. He was not an old nobleman who was very easily bewildered, because he had seen a great deal of the world; but here was something he found so novel that it almost took his lordly breath away, and caused him some singular emotions. He had never cared for children; he had been so occupied with his own pleasures that he had never had time to care for them. His own sons had not interested him when they were very young – though sometimes he remembered having thought Cedric's father a handsome and strong little fellow. He had been so selfish himself that he had missed the pleasure of seeing unselfishness in others, and he had not known how tender and faithful and affectionate a kind-hearted little child can be, and how innocent and unconscious are its simple, generous impulses. A boy had always seemed to him a most objectionable little animal, selfish and greedy and boisterous when not under strict restraint; his own two eldest sons had given their tutors constant trouble and annoyance, and of the younger one he fancied he had heard few complaints because the boy was of no particular importance. It had never once occurred to him that he should like his grandson; he had sent for the little Cedric because his pride impelled him to do so. If the boy was to take his place in the future, he did not wish his name to be ridiculous by descending to an uneducated boor. He had been convinced the boy would be a clownish fellow if he were brought up in America. He had no feeling of affection for the lad, his only hope was that he should find him decently well featured and with a respectable share of sense; he had been so disappointed in his other sons, and had been made so furious by Captain Errol's American marriage, that he had never once thought that anything creditable could come of it. When the footman had announced Lord Fauntleroy he had almost dreaded to look at the boy lest he should find him all he had feared. It was because of this feeling that he had ordered that the child should be sent to him alone. His pride could not endure that others should see his disappointment if he was to be disappointed. His proud, stubborn old heart therefore had leaped within him when the boy came forward with his graceful easy carriage, his fearless hand on the big dog's neck. Even in the moments when he had hoped the most, the Earl had never hoped that his grandson would look like that. It seemed almost too good to be true that this should be the boy he had dreaded to see – the child of the woman he so disliked – this little fellow with so much beauty and such a brave, childish grace! The Earl's stern composure was quite shaken by this startling surprise.

Grandad

When we go over
to my grandad's
he falls asleep

While he's asleep
he snores.

When he wakes up,
he says,
'Did I snore?
did I snore?
did I snore?'

Everybody says, 'No,
you didn't snore.'

Why do we lie to him?

Michael Rosen

Mr Tom Narrow

A scandalous man
  Was Mr Tom Narrow
He pushed his grandmother
  Round in a barrow.
And he called out loud
  As he rang his bell,
'Grannies to sell!
  Old grannies to sell!'

The neighbours said,
  As they passed them by,
'This poor old lady
  We will not buy.
He surely must be
  A mischievous man
To try for to sell
  His own dear Gran.'

'Besides,' said another,
  'If you ask me,
She'd be very small use
  That I can see.'
'You're right,' said a third,
  'And no mistake –
A very poor bargain
  She'd surely make.'

So Mr Tom Narrow
   He scratched his head,
And he sent his grandmother
   Back to bed;
And he rang his bell
   Through all the town
Till he sold his barrow
   For half a crown.

Eleanor Farjeon

ROALD DAHL

FROM Charlie and the Chocolate Factory

Perhaps the best-known grandparents of all are
Grandpa Joe and Grandma Josephine, Grandpa
George and Grandma Georgina who lived next door
to Willy Wonka's chocolate factory.

*   *   *

In the evenings, after he had finished his supper of watery
cabbage soup, Charlie always went into the room of his
four grandparents to listen to their stories, and then afterwards to say good night.

Every one of these old people was over ninety. They
were as shrivelled as prunes, and as bony as skeletons, and
throughout the day, until Charlie made his appearance,
they lay huddled in their one bed, two at either end, with
nightcaps on to keep their heads warm, dozing the time
away with nothing to do. But as soon as they heard the
door opening, and heard Charlie's voice saying, 'Good
evening, Grandpa Joe and Grandma Josephine, and
Grandpa George and Grandma Georgina,' then all four of
them would suddenly sit up, and their old wrinkled faces
would light up with smiles of pleasure – and the talking
would begin. For they loved this little boy. He was the only
bright thing in their lives, and his evening visits were
something that they looked forward to all day long. Often,
Charlie's mother and father would come in as well and

stand by the door, listening to the stories that the old people told; and thus, for perhaps half an hour every night, this room would become a happy place, and the whole family would forget that it was hungry and poor.

One evening, when Charlie went in to see his grandparents, he said to them, 'Is it *really* true that Wonka's Chocolate Factory is the biggest in the world?'

'*True?*' cried all four of them at once. 'Of course it's true! Good heavens, didn't you know *that?* It's about *fifty* times as big as any other!'

'And is Mr Willy Wonka *really* the cleverest chocolate maker in the world?'

'My *dear* boy,' said Grandpa Joe, raising himself up a little higher on his pillow, 'Mr Willy Wonka is the most *amazing*, the most *fantastic*, the most *extraordinary* chocolate maker the world has ever seen! I thought *everybody* knew that!'

'I knew he was famous, Grandpa Joe, and I knew he was very clever . . .'

'*Clever*!' cried the old man. 'He's more than that! He's a *magician* with chocolate! He can make *anything* – anything he wants! Isn't that a fact, my dears?'

The other three old people nodded their heads slowly up and down, and said, '*Absolutely* true. *Just* as true as can be.'

And Grandpa Joe said, 'You mean to say I've never *told* you about Mr Willy Wonka and his factory?'

'Never,' answered little Charlie.

'Good heavens above! I don't know what's the matter with me!'

'Will you tell me now, Grandpa Joe, please?'

'I certainly will. Sit down beside me on the bed, my dear, and listen carefully.'

Grandpa Joe was the oldest of the four grandparents. He was ninety-six and a half, and that is just about as old as anybody can be. Like all extremely old people, he was delicate and weak, and throughout the day he spoke very little. But in the evenings, when Charlie, his beloved grandson, was in the room, he seemed in some marvellous way to grow quite young again. All his tiredness fell away from him, and he became as eager and excited as a young boy.

'Oh, what a man he is, this Mr Willy Wonka!' cried Grandpa Joe. 'Did you know, for example, that he has himself invented more than two hundred new kinds of chocolate bars, each with a different centre, each far sweeter and creamier and more delicious than anything the other chocolate factories can make!'

'Perfectly true!' cried Grandma Josephine. 'And he sends them to *all* the four corners of the earth! Isn't that so, Grandpa Joe?'

'It is, my dear, it is. And to all the kings and presidents

of the world as well. But it isn't only chocolate bars that he makes. Oh, dear me, no! He has some really *fantastic* inventions up his sleeve, Mr Willy Wonka has! Did you know that he's invented a way of making chocolate ice cream so that it stays cold for hours and hours without being in the refrigerator? You can even leave it lying in the sun all morning on a hot day and it won't go runny!'

'But that's *impossible*!' said little Charlie, staring at his grandfather.

As Fit as a Fiddle

Grandfather George is as fit as a fiddle,
As fit as a fiddle right up from his middle,
Grandfather George is as fit as a fiddle,
As fit as a fiddle right down to his toes.

Grandfather George, whenever I meet him
Nips my right ear and asks me a riddle,
And when Mother questions him how he is keeping,
He slaps his left leg and says 'Fit as a fiddle!'

Once I said 'Grandfather George, why a fiddle,
Why is a fiddle especially fit?'
He laughed very loud and said 'Hey diddle-diddle,
I'll give you a sixpence if you'll answer that!'

So now I ask everyone, friends and relations,
People I talk to wherever I go,
I ask them on buses, in shops and at stations:
I suppose, by the way, that you do not know?

Pauline Clarke

My Grandad's Old

My grandad's old
And lost his hair
And that's why flies
Are landing there.

Spike Milligan

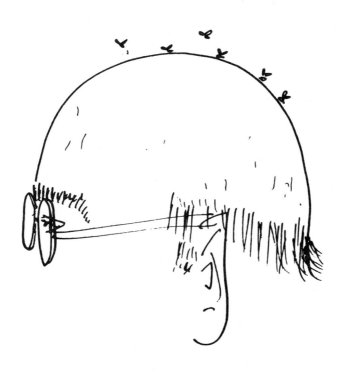

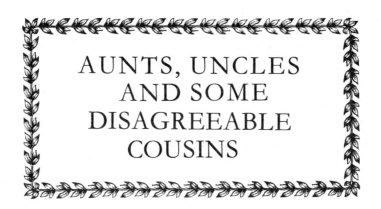

AUNTS, UNCLES
AND SOME
DISAGREEABLE
COUSINS

There's a wonderful variety to be found amongst aunts, often more good than bad. They turn up from far-flung places with mysterious presents, offer unusual holidays, or give homes to abandoned children. But uncles are a different matter: sometimes exciting, sometimes funny and sometimes really nasty. For instance, read about Christina's crippled Uncle Russell in *Flambards*, or the Wicked Duke in *The Thirteen Clocks*.

JAMES THURBER

FROM The Thirteen Clocks

Once upon a time, in a gloomy castle on a lonely hill, where there were thirteen clocks that wouldn't go, there lived a cold, aggressive Duke, and his niece, the Princess Saralinda. She was warm in every wind and weather, but he was always cold. His hands were as cold as his smile and almost as cold as his heart. He wore gloves when he was asleep, and he wore gloves when he was awake, which made it difficult for him to pick up pins or coins or the kernels of nuts, or to tear the wings from nightingales. He was six feet four, and forty-six, and even colder than he thought he was. One eye wore a velvet patch; the other glittered through a monocle, which made half his body seem closer to you than the other half. He had lost one eye when he was twelve, for he was fond of peering into nests and lairs in search of birds and animals to maul. One afternoon, a mother shrike had mauled him first. His nights were spent in evil dreams, and his days were given to wicked schemes.

Wickedly scheming, he would limp and cackle through the cold corridors of the castle, planning new impossible feats for the suitors of Saralinda to perform. He did not wish to give her hand in marriage, since her hand was the only warm hand in the castle. Even the hands of his watch and the hands of all the thirteen clocks were frozen. They

had all frozen at the same time, on a snowy night, seven years before, and after that it was always ten minutes to five in the castle. Travellers and mariners would look up at the gloomy castle on the lonely hill and say, 'Time lies frozen there. It's always Then. It's never Now.'

The cold Duke was afraid of Now, for Now has warmth and urgency, and Then is dead and buried. Now might bring a certain knight of gay and shining courage – 'But, no!' the cold Duke muttered. 'The Prince will break himself against a new and awful labour: a place too high to reach, a thing too far to find, a burden too heavy to lift.' The Duke was afraid of Now, but he tampered with the clocks to see if they would go, out of a strange perversity, praying that they wouldn't. Tinkers and tinkerers and a few wizards who happened by tried to start the clocks with tools or magic words, or by shaking them and cursing, but nothing whirred or ticked. The clocks were dead, and in the end, brooding on it, the Duke decided he had murdered time, slain it with his sword, and wiped his bloody blade upon its beard and left it lying there, bleeding hours and minutes, its springs uncoiled and sprawling, its pendulum disintegrating.

The Duke limped because his legs were of different lengths. The right one had outgrown the left because, when he was young, he had spent his mornings place-kicking pups and punting kittens. He would say to a suitor, 'What is the difference in the length of my legs?' and if the youth replied, 'Why, one is shorter than the other,' the Duke would run him through with the sword he carried in his sword-cane and feed him to the geese. The suitor was supposed to say, 'Why, one is longer than the other.' Many a prince had been run through for naming the wrong difference.

Aunts and Uncles

When Aunty Jane
Became a Crane
She put one leg behind her head;
And even when the clock struck ten
Refused to go to bed.

When Aunty Grace
Became a Plaice
She all but vanished sideways on;
Except her nose
And pointed toes
The rest of her was gone.

When Uncle Wog
Became a Dog
He hid himself for shame;
He sometimes hid his bone as well
And wouldn't hear the front-door bell,
Or answer to his name.

When Uncle Jake
Became a Snake
He never found it out;
And so as no one mentions it
One sees him still about.

Mervyn Peake

K. M. PEYTON

FROM Flambards

Christina, who is an orphan, goes to live with her
uncle and two cousins, William and Mark, at an old
country house called Flambards. She quickly finds out
that old Mr Russell is a dreadful bully.

*   *   *

Russell dismissed Dick. Christina went to the door with
him, and was surprised to find a man standing there,
pressing the doorbell.

'Mr William Russell live here, miss?'

'Yes.'

The man handed her a parcel. 'With the regards of Mr
Dermot,' he said and, touching his cap, walked away down
the drive.

Christina took the parcel back into the library and
handed it to her uncle. 'A man delivered this, with the
regards of Mr Dermot.'

'Who the devil's Mr Dermot?' Russell said, with a glare
at the parcel.

'He didn't say.'

'Open it, girl.'

Christina did as she was told, and was shocked by her
own stupidity. For the parcel was a book called *A Scientific
Statement of the Progress of Aeronautical Science up to the
Present Time*, and on the fly-leaf a small hand had written,

'To help while away the time.' It was for William upstairs, not his father.

She said, 'It's for William.'

'Show me,' said Russell.

Christina handed it over reluctantly. She had a feeling that William would have preferred to keep his reading-matter private. Russell stared at the title.

'Good God, what's this stuff?'

Mark leaned over the back of the chair to read the cover, and laughed. 'That's Will's passion. Flying.'

'*Flying*!' Russell was disgusted. He opened the book and read the inscription. 'I'll give him something to while away his time! I've never seen him show any interest in my books, the brainless puppy! Who is this Dermot, filling his head with rubbish? Eh, Mark? You know him?'

'Never heard of him,' said Mark.

'Holy Moses, if he wants to while away his time' – Russell was thumping about, stumbling over to the bookcase, red with anger – 'I'll give him something. Here, Christina, take these out. I'll give him reading-matter. Take this up to him, and this one. Here. And this.'

Christina took the awkward tomes, silent with horror. They were *The Breeding of Foxhounds*, *Baily's Hunting Directory*, *Observations on Fox-hunting*, *Thoughts on Hunting*, *The Essex Foxhounds*, and *Goodall's Practice with Foxhounds*.

'Take him those! Go on! With my compliments. I'll see he gets his reading-matter. And when he's finished those I'll send him some more.' He took the slim volume on flying and threw it on the fire, where it burst into merry flames. Christina could not restrain a gasp of dismay, and even Mark looked disconcerted.

'Oh, I say, Father.'

Russell aimed a great swipe at Mark with his crutch, which Mark avoided with a quick, practised sidestep.

'Get out, both of you! Get upstairs with those, girl, and
tell Will to start reading. Get out of my sight before I tan
the hides off you!'

He was scarlet with passion, crashing his crutches in the
hearth, poking the flying-book deeper into the fire.
Christina, clutching her load of books, hurried out, and
Mark opened the door for her, grinning.

'Phew! What a paddy!'

Once in the hall, Christina burst into tears. She could
not wipe her eyes for the books, and stood gulping un-
controllably. 'It's – it's not fair! The – the – book was for
– for Will! It's all – my fault!'

'Oh, Will's used to it,' Mark said. 'Don't upset yourself,
we're always like this here. You just have to keep out of
the old man's way till he's over it.'

To her amazement, Mark was not the least concerned.
Christina was outraged, and horrified by her own part in
the matter. It need never have happened at all, if she had
not been so dull-witted. Her heart ached for poor helpless
William as she lugged the books up the stairs. Mark had
already washed his hands of the incident and gone out of
the front door with the foxhounds at his heels. Christina's

sense of injustice choked her. She fumbled for William's doorknob, and backed into the room with her burden, the sobs still shaking in her throat.

'Whatever's all that?' William asked cheerfully.

'For – for you!'

'What's the matter? What's wrong?'

Christina set the pile of books on the chair beside William's bed, and told him what had happened. As she had expected, William's rage turned itself on her. She buried her head in the bedclothes and sobbed: 'I'm sorry! I didn't know he was so awful!'

'Oh, look, I'm sorry too,' William said, immediately embarrassed by her despair. 'It wasn't your fault. Oh, look, please don't cry, else I shall too.'

He gave her a white, desolate look, biting his lip with disappointment. His glance passed on to the gold-tooled hunting-books, and a look of utter contempt came into his face.

'If he thinks I'm going to read that rubbish! I'd – I'd like to tear them into shreds! If only I had the nerve –'

'Oh, William, don't make it worse! Don't be so stupid.'

Christina pulled herself together and wiped her eyes. William lay back, glaring at the ceiling, his lips tight. His face was very pale, and there were dark shadows under his eyes. Christina said nervously, 'Who is Mr Dermot, then?'

'A friend,' said William distantly.

Later that evening Russell sent a message up to William to the effect that when he came downstairs, he was going to answer questions on the hunting-books, and if he could not answer correctly, he would get a flogging, smashed knee or no smashed knee. William picked up *Baily's Hunting Directory* and threw it across the room, where it landed under the washstand, half its leaves bursting out across the floor.

Hugger Mugger

I'd sooner be
Jumped and thumped and dumped,

I'd sooner be
slugged and mugged . . . than hugged . . .

And clobbered with a slobbering
Kiss by my Auntie Jean
You know what I mean:

Whenever she comes to stay
you know you're bound
to get one
A quick
   short
   peck
   would
   be
   OK
But this is a
Whacking great
Smacking great
Wet one!
All whoosh and spit
And crunch and squeeze
And '*Dear* little boy!'
And 'Auntie's missed you!'
And 'Come to Auntie, she
Hasn't *kissed* you!'
Please don't do it, Auntie,
PLEASE!

Or if you've absolutely
Got to,

And nothing on *earth* can persuade you
Not to,

The trick
Is to make it
Quick,

You know what I mean?
For as things are,
I really would far,

Far sooner be
Jumped and thumped and dumped,

I'd sooner be
Slugged and mugged . . . than *hugged* . . .

And clobbered with a slobbering
Kiss by my Auntie

Jean!

Kit Wright

DIANA WYNNE JONES

FROM Eight Days of Luke

David has to live with three elderly cousins who don't like him. This is the first day of his holidays.

*   *   *

The hall was empty. This meant that, because of the railway work-to-rule, his trunk had not arrived yet. That was a nuisance. David's cricket-bat and the only pair of trousers that still fitted him had been in that trunk. It meant borrowing a bat and being stuck with short, tight school trousers until it arrived. He was rather sadly looking at the empty space in the hall where his trunk usually stood, when the door of the study opened. Cousin Ronald, balder and stouter and busier-looking than ever, came hurrying out, and with him came a gush of cricket-commentary from the radio in the study.

David remembered his six triumphant wickets. 'Oh, Cousin Ronald, do you know what!' he said happily.

Cousin Ronald seemed dumbfounded. He stopped in his tracks and stared at David. 'What are *you* doing here?' he said.

'It's holidays. We broke up yesterday,' David said. 'But do you know what –?'

'Oh, this is too bad!' Cousin Ronald interrupted peevishly. 'And I suppose they've sent you home early because of some blasted epidemic and we'll all catch it now.'

'No. Honestly,' protested David. 'It's just the end of term.' He was beginning to lose all his joy in telling Cousin Ronald about those wickets; but it was too fine not to tell, so he tried again. 'And do you know —?'

'It *can't* be the end of term!' said Cousin Ronald. 'Not already, boy.'

'Well, it is,' said David.

'What a counfounded nuisance!' Cousin Ronald exclaimed, and plunged back into the study again and shut himself and the cricket commentary away inside it.

More than a little dashed, David went slowly away upstairs, trying not to feel miserable, trying to think about the cricket books in his bedroom. He came across Uncle Bernard on the first landing. Uncle Bernard did not seem to see David. He just tottered away to the bathroom looking frail and vague. David was heartily relieved. When Uncle Bernard noticed him, he always noticed the colour of David's fingernails, the length of his hair and the fact that his tie was comfortably in his pocket. It was much better not to be noticed by Uncle Bernard. David turned thankfully to go up the second flight of stairs and found Aunt Dot's tall figure coming down them.

'David!' exclaimed Aunt Dot. 'Whatever are you doing *here*?'

'It's the holidays,' David explained once more. 'We broke up yesterday.'

'Broke up *yesterday*!' said Aunt Dot. 'I thought there was another week to go. It was extremely thoughtless of you not to let me know.' Since David knew that the school always sent Aunt Dot a list of terms and holidays, he said nothing. 'What a nuisance!' said Aunt Dot. 'Well, since you're here, David, go and wash and I'll see Mrs Thirsk. Supper's in half an hour.' She came on downstairs. David, knowing what a point Aunt Dot made of politeness, stood aside to let her pass. But Aunt Dot stopped again. 'Good gracious, David!' she said. 'Whose clothes are you wearing?'

'No one's,' said David. 'Mine, I mean.'

'They've shrunk abominably,' said Aunt Dot. 'I shall write to the school and complain.'

'Oh, please don't,' said David. 'It's not the clothes – really. I think I grew very fast or something.'

'Nobody grows that fast,' Aunt Dot decreed. 'Those clothes were a good fit at Easter. You must go straight upstairs and see if you have anything else to wear. You can't come to supper looking like that.' And she sailed away downstairs.

David went on up to his bare, tidy bedroom. While he searched for clothes, he could not help forlornly wondering whether any of his school friends were having such a cheerless homecoming as he was. He rather thought that most of them had parents and brothers and things who were actually glad to see them. Some of the lucky so-and-sos even had dogs. David would have liked a dog above all things. But the thought of Uncle Bernard being asked to countenance a dog was almost frightening.

The only clothes he could find were smaller than the ones he had on. When Mrs Thirsk rang the gong, David was forced to go down to supper as he was. He met Mrs Thirsk in the passage and she looked him over with utter contempt.

'You do look a proper scarecrow,' she said. 'Your Uncle's going to have something to say about that hair of yours, if I know anything about anything.'

'Yes, but you don't,' said David.

'Don't what?' said Mrs Thirsk.

'Know anything about anything,' said David, and he escaped into the dining-room, feeling a little better for having annoyed Mrs Thirsk. He had been at war with

Mrs Thirsk from the moment he came to live in Uncle Bernard's house. Mrs Thirsk hated boys. David loathed every inch of Mrs Thirsk, from her blank square face to her blunt square feet. So he smiled a little as he slipped into the dining-room.

The smile vanished when he found Astrid there. Astrid was sitting beside the french windows with her feet up, because, as everyone knew only too well, her health was bad. Astrid was quite pretty. She had fairish hair and big blue eyes, but her face was always pale and peevish, or it would have looked prettier. She dressed very smartly and told everyone she was twenty-five – she had been telling everyone this, to David's certain knowledge, for six years now.

At the sight of David, she gave a cry of dismay. 'Never tell me you're back already! Oh, this is *too* bad! Ronald, you might have warned me!' she said, as Cousin Ronald came in.

Cousin Ronald was carrying a sheet of paper which David recognized as the list of holiday dates that the school had sent last autumn. 'It came as a shock to me too,' he said. 'But they do seem to give the twentieth here.'

'But you told me the twenty-eighth!' Astrid said indignantly.

Aunt Dot came in at this moment, with her diary open in front of her nose. David drifted away to the other end of the room. 'Ronald,' said Aunt Dot, 'I have the end of term down here clearly as the twenty-eighth. Why was I misinformed?'

'Trust Ronald to get it wrong!' said Astrid. 'If we have to miss going to Scarborough because of this, I don't know what I shall do. One of my heads is coming on already.'

David, having no wish to hear any more about Astrid's

head, reached out and gently twiddled the knobs of the radio on the sideboard. He was in luck. An announcer said: 'Now, cricket. England in the Third Test are –'

'David!' said Aunt Dot. 'People are talking. Turn that off at once.'

Sighing, David turned the knob and silenced the announcer. But, at the same moment, Cousin Ronald hurried across the room, saying irritably: 'I tell you I've no idea how it happened!' and snapped the radio on again.

'Five wickets for fourteen runs,' said the radio.

'Quiet,' Cousin Ronald said severely. 'I have to know how England are doing against the Australians.'

To David's secret indignation, no one made the slightest objection. Everyone stopped talking while the radio told them that England were 112 for eight when rain stopped play. By this time Uncle Bernard had tottered in, still frail from finding David had come home, and Mrs Thirsk was bringing in a tray of thick brown soup. Everyone sat down and began to eat. The thick brown soup tasted thick and brown.

All this while, Uncle Bernard had been hovering on the edge of the action, waiting for an opening. Now, just as Mrs Thirsk came to bring pudding, he pounced. 'Growing,' he said. 'And I suppose you can't help your hair growing either? You must have it cut at once, boy.' The odd thing about Uncle Bernard was that when he attacked David he never seemed in the least frail or ill. 'Hanging round your ears in that unmanly way!' he said vigorously. 'I'm surprised they haven't made you have it cut at school.'

Mrs Thirsk shot David a malicious, meaning look, and David was naturally forced to defend himself. 'The other boys all have hair much longer than this,' he said. 'No one minds these days. Uncle Bernard.'

'Well I do mind,' said Uncle Bernard. 'I'm ashamed to look at you. You'll have it all off on Monday.'

'No,' said David. 'I –'

'*What?*' said Uncle Bernard. 'Do you have the face to contradict me? Boys do not decide the length of their hair, let me tell you. Their guardians do. And boys do not contradict their guardians, David.'

'I'm not really contradicting,' David said earnestly. Because Mrs Thirsk was there, he was desperately set on winning, but he knew that he dared not seem rude or ungrateful. 'It's just that I want to grow my hair, Uncle Bernard. And it'll cost less money if I don't have it cut, won't it?'

'Money,' said Uncle Bernard unfairly, 'is no object with me when it's a question of right and wrong. And it is *wrong* for you to be seen with hair that length.'

'Not these days,' David explained politely. 'It's the fashion you see, and it really isn't wrong. I expect you're a bit out of date, Uncle Bernard.' He smiled kindly and, he hoped, firmly at Uncle Bernard, and was a little put out to hear Astrid snorting with laughter across the table.

'I never heard such a thing!' said Uncle Bernard. Then he went frail and added pathetically: 'And I hope I shall never hear such a thing again.'

David, to his amazement, saw that he was winning. He had Uncle Bernard on the run. It was so unheard of that, for a moment, David could not think of anything to say that would clinch his victory. And while he wondered, Mrs Thirsk turned his success into total failure.

'Yes,' she said, 'and did you ever *see* such a thing as this, either?' Triumphantly, she placed a small mat with crochet edging in front of Uncle Bernard. In the middle of the mat, very thoroughly stuck to it, was a wad of something pink and rather shiny, with teeth-marks in it.

Uncle Bernard peered at it. 'What is this?' he said.

'David can tell you,' said Mrs Thirsk, throwing David another malicious look.

Uncle Bernard, frail and puzzled, looked up at David.

'It's chewing-gum,' David confessed wretchedly. How it had got stuck to the mat on his dressing-table, he could not imagine. He supposed he must have put it down there while he was hunting for clothes. But he knew it was all up for him now.

'Chewing-gum? In *my* house!' said Uncle Bernard.

'How simply filthy!' said Aunt Dot.

Astrid and Cousin Ronald closed in again then too, while Mrs Thirsk, looking like the Triumph of Righteousness, briskly planked a plate of stiff, cold chocolate pudding in front of David. Such of it as David managed to eat tasted as thick and brown as the rest of supper. As the row went on, as all four of his relations continued to clamour how disgusting he was and Mrs Thirsk to shoot smug looks at him, David resolved bitterly, vengefully, that if it was the last thing he did, he would tell Mrs Thirsk how rotten her food was.

It ended with David being sent up to bed. By that time he was quite glad to go.

CHARLOTTE BRONTË

FROM Jane Eyre

There are many stories of the terrible times orphaned
Jane Eyre had when she was a poor relation in the
house of Aunt Reed, so it's good to read how she
stood up to her awful cousin John.

*   *   *

With Bewick on my knee, I was then happy: happy at least
in my way. I feared nothing but interruption, and that
came too soon. The breakfast-room door was opened.

'Boh! Madam Mope!' cried the voice of John Reed; then
he paused: he found the room apparently empty.

'Where the dickens is she?' he continued. 'Lizzy! Georgy!
(calling to his sisters) Jane is not here: tell mamma she is
run out into the rain – bad animal!'

'It is well I drew the curtain,' thought I, and I wished
fervently he might not discover my hiding-place: nor would
John Reed have found it out himself; he was not quick
either of vision or conception; but Eliza just put her head
in at the door, and said at once: 'She is in the window-seat,
to be sure, Jack.'

And I came out immediately, for I trembled at the idea
of being dragged forth by the said Jack.

'What do you want?' I asked with awkward diffidence.

'Say, "what do you want, Master Reed",' was the
answer. 'I want you to come here'; and seating himself in

an arm-chair, he intimated by a gesture that I was to approach and stand before him.

John Reed was a schoolboy of fourteen years old; four years older than I, for I was but ten; large and stout for his age, with a dingy and unwholesome skin; thick lineaments in a spacious visage, heavy limbs and large extremities. He gorged himself habitually at table, which made him bilious, and gave him a dim and bleared eye with flabby cheeks. He ought now to have been at school; but his mamma had taken him home for a month or two, 'on account of his delicate health'. Mr Miles, the master, affirmed that he would do very well if he had fewer cakes and sweetmeats sent him from home; but the mother's heart turned from an opinion so harsh, and inclined rather to the more refined idea that John's sallowness was owing to over-application, and, perhaps, to pining after home.

John had not much affection for his mother and sisters, and an antipathy to me. He bullied and punished me; not two or three times in the week, nor once or twice in a day, but continually: every nerve I had feared him, and every morsel of flesh on my bones shrank when he came near. There were moments when I was bewildered by the terror he inspired, because I had no appeal whatever against either his menaces or his inflictions; the servants did not like to offend their young master by taking my part against him, and Mrs Reed was blind and deaf on the subject: she never saw him strike or heard him abuse me, though he did both now and then in her very presence; more frequently, however, behind her back.

Habitually obedient to John, I came up to his chair: he spent some three minutes in thrusting out his tongue at me as far as he could without damaging the roots: I knew he would soon strike, and while dreading the blow, I mused on the disgusting and ugly appearance of him who would presently deal it. I wonder if he read that notion in my face; for, all at once, without speaking, he struck suddenly and strongly. I tottered, and on regaining my equilibrium retired back a step or two from his chair.

'That is for your impudence in answering mamma a while since,' said he, 'and for your sneaking way of getting behind curtains, and for the look you had in your eyes two minutes since, you rat!'

Accustomed to John Reed's abuse, I never had an idea of replying to it: my care was how to endure the blow which would certainly follow the insult.

'What were you doing behind the curtain?' he asked.

'I was reading.'

'Show the book.'

I returned to the window and fetched it thence.

'You have no business to take our books; you are a dependant, mamma says; you have no money; your father left you none; you ought to beg, and not to live here with gentlemen's children like us, and eat the same meals we do, and wear clothes at our mamma's expense. Now, I'll teach you to rummage my book-shelves: for they *are* mine; all the house belongs to me, or will do in a few years. Go and stand by the door, out of the way of the mirror and the windows.'

I did so, not at first aware what was his intention; but when I saw him lift and poise the book and stand in act to hurl it, I instinctively started aside with a cry of alarm: not soon enough, however; the volume was flung, it hit me, and I fell, striking my head against the door and cutting it. The cut bled, the pain was sharp: my terror had passed its climax; other feelings succeeded.

'Wicked and cruel boy!' I said. 'You are like a murderer – you are like a slave-driver – you are like the Roman emperors!'

I had read Goldsmith's *History of Rome*, and had formed my opinion of Nero, Caligula, &c. Also I had drawn parallels in silence, which I never thought thus to have declared aloud.

'What! what!' he cried. 'Did she say that to me? Did you hear her, Eliza and Georgiana? Won't I tell mamma? but first –'

He ran headlong at me: I felt him grasp my hair and my shoulder: he had closed with a desperate thing. I really saw in him a tyrant: a murderer. I felt a drop or two of blood from my head trickle down my neck, and was sensible of somewhat pungent suffering: these sensations for the time predominated over fear, and I received him in frantic sort. I don't very well know what I did with my hands, but he called me 'Rat! rat!' and bellowed out aloud. Aid was near him: Eliza and Georgiana had run for Mrs Reed, who was gone upstairs; she now came upon the scene, followed by Bessie and her maid Abbot. We were parted: I heard the words –

'Dear! dear! What a fury to fly at Master John!'

'Did ever anybody see such a picture of passion!'

Then Mrs Reed subjoined: 'Take her away to the red-room, and lock her in there.' Four hands were immediately laid upon me, and I was borne upstairs.

Family Album

I wish I liked Aunt Leonora
When she draws in her breath with a hiss
And with fingers of ice and a grip like a vice
She gives me a walloping kiss.

I wish I loved Uncle Nathaniel
(The one with the teeth and the snore).
He's really a pain when he tells me *again*
About what he did in the War.

I really don't care for Aunt Millie,
Her bangles and brooches and beads,
Or the gun that she shoots or those ex-army boots
Or the terrible dogs that she breeds.

I simply can't stand Uncle Albert.
Quite frankly, he fills me with dread
When he gives us a tune with a knife, fork and spoon.
(I don't think he's right in the head.)

I wish I loved Hetty and Harry
(Aunt Hilary's horrible twins)
As they lie in their cots giving off lots and lots
Of gurgles and gargles and grins.

As for nieces or nephews or cousins
There seems nothing else one can do
Except sit in a chair and exchange a cold stare
As if we came out of a Zoo.

Though they say blood is thicker than water,
I'm not at all certain it's so.
If you think it's the case, kindly write to this space.
It's something I'm anxious to know.

If we only could choose our relations
How happy, I'm certain, we'd be!
And just one thing more: I am perfectly sure
Mine all feel the same about me.

Charles Causley

NOEL STREATFEILD

FROM The Growing Summer

A family of children used to an ordinary, comfortable way of living are suddenly packed off to Ireland to stay with an unknown aunt who isn't like anyone they've ever known.

All Noel Streatfeild's books have aunts in them, but I think Aunt Dymphna is the best.

*　　　*　　　*

The first impression of Great-Aunt Dymphna was that she was more like an enormous bird than a great-aunt. This was partly because she wore a black cape, which seemed to flap behind her when she moved. Then her nose stuck out of her thin wrinkled old face just like a very hooked beak. On her head she wore a man's tweed hat beneath which straggled wispy white hair. She wore under the cape a shapeless long black dress. On her feet, in spite of it being a fine warm evening, were rubber boots.

The children gazed at their great-aunt, so startled by her appearance that the polite greetings they would have made vanished from their minds. Naomi was so scared that, though tears went on rolling down her cheeks, she did not make any more noise. Great-Aunt Dymphna had turned her attention to the luggage.

'Clutter, clutter! I could never abide clutter. What have

you got in all this?' As she said 'this' a rubber boot kicked
at the nearest suitcase.

'Clothes mostly,' said Alex.

'Mummy didn't know what we'd need,' Penny explained,
'so she said we'd have to bring everything.'

'Well, as it's here we must take it home I suppose,' said
Great-Aunt Dymphna. 'Bring it to the car,' and she turned
and, like a great black eagle, swept out.

Both at London airport and when they had arrived at
Cork a porter had helped with the luggage. But now there
was no porter in sight and it was clear Great-Aunt Dymphna
did not expect that one would be used. Alex took charge.

'You and Naomi carry those two small cases,' he said to
Robin. 'If you could manage one of the big ones, Penny, I
can take both mine and then I'll come back for the rest.'

Afterwards the children could never remember much
about the drive to Reenmore. Great-Aunt Dymphna, in a
terrifyingly erratic way, drove the car. It was a large
incredibly old black Austin. As the children lurched and

bounced along – Robin in front, the other three in the back – Great-Aunt Dymphna shot out information about what they met in passing.

'Never trust cows when there's a human with them. Plenty of sense when on their own. Nearly hit that one but only because that stupid man directed the poor beast the wrong way.'

As they flashed past farms dogs ran out barking, prepared at risk of their lives to run beside the car.

'Never alter course for a dog,' Great-Aunt Dymphna shouted, 'just tell him where you are going. It's all he wants.' Then, to the dog: 'We are going to Reenmore, dear.' Her system worked for at once the dog stopped barking and quietly ran back home.

For other cars or for bicycles she had no respect at all.

'Road hogs,' she roared. 'Road hogs. Get out of my way or be smashed, that's my rule.'

'Oh, Penny,' Naomi whispered, clinging to her. 'We'll be killed, I know we will.'

Penny was sure Naomi was right but she managed to sound brave.

'I expect it's all right. She's been driving all her life and she's still alive.'

The only road-users Great-Aunt Dymphna respected were what the children would have called gipsies, but which she called tinkers. They passed a cavalcade of these travelling, not in the gipsy caravans they had seen in England, but in a different type with rounded tops. Behind and in front of the caravans horses ran loose.

'Splendid people tinkers,' Great-Aunt Dymphna shouted. Then, slowing down, she called out something to the tinkers which might, for all the children understood, have been in a foreign language. Then, to the children: 'If you need medicine they'll tell you where it grows.'

Alex took advantage of the car slowing down to mention the cable.

'We promised Mummy we'd send it,' he explained. 'And she's sending one to us to say she's arrived and how Daddy is.'

'Perhaps a creamery lorry will deliver it sometime,' Great-Aunt Dymphna said. 'That's the only way a telegram reaches me. You can send yours from Bantry. The post office will be closed but you can telephone from the hotel.'

Penny had no idea what a creamery lorry might be but she desperately wanted her mother's cable.

'Oh, dear, I hope the creamery lorry will be quick, we do so dreadfully want to know how Daddy is.'

'Holding his own,' Great-Aunt Dymphna shouted. 'I asked the seagulls before I came out. They'll tell me if there's any change.'

'She's as mad as a coot,' Alex whispered to Penny. 'I should think she ought to be in an asylum.'

Penny shivered.

'I do hope other people live close to Reenmore. I don't like us to be alone with her.'

But in Bantry when they stopped to send the cable nobody seemed to think Great-Aunt Dymphna mad. It is true the children understood very little of what was said for they were not used to the Irish brogue, but it was clear from the tone of voice used and the expression on people's faces that what the people of Bantry felt was respect. It came from the man who filled the car up with petrol, and another who put some parcels in the boot.

'Extraordinary!' Alex whispered to Penny when he came out of the hotel. 'When I said "Miss Gareth said it would be all right to send a cable" you'd have thought I had said the Queen had said it was all right.'

'Why, what did they say?' Penny asked.

'It was more the way they said it than what they said, but they told me to write down the message and they would telephone it through right away.'

It was beginning to get dark when they left Bantry but as the children peered out of the windows they could just see purplish mountains, and that the roads had fuchsia hedges instead of ordinary bushes, and that they must be ponds or lakes for often they caught the shimmer of water.

'At least it's awfully pretty,' Penny whispered to Alex. 'Like Mummy said it would be.'

'I can't see how that'll help if she's mad,' Alex whispered back.

Suddenly, without a word of warning, Great-Aunt Dymphna stopped the car.

'We're home.' Then she chuckled. 'I expect you poor little town types thought we'd never make it, but we always do. You'll learn.'

JANE GARDAM

Auntie Kitty and the Fever House
FROM A Few Fair Days

Here's a strange aunt who turned up just in time to
help stop her niece Lucy from being very unhappy.

* * *

Whenever Lucy's mother had been away before, which was
almost never, and then only overnight to Scarborough or
Whitby, she had always sent Lucy a postcard. But now,
morning after morning, there was no post waiting on her
breakfast plate. Lucy grew quiet.

One day she told Phyllis she wasn't going on the
afternoon walk. Phyllis went so fast and so far and in the
teeth of the wind to give the baby good strong air which
Lucy hated. She hated all walks with the baby because
people would stop and look at him and he was very ugly.
(He grew beautiful later.)

'*Can't* I stay?'

'An' what'll you do?'

'I'll just play. I'll play actresses.'

'Well, doant set place afire. And lock't doors.' And she
was off, full steam ahead.

Lucy locked the front door. Then she went to the
kitchen and locked the back door. She got up in a chair
and looked into the kitchen mirror. She made a proud and
cruel face. 'I am the Princess of Cleves,' she said. She got
down from the chair and leaning over the small fire she

262

blacked her fingers with the soot at the fire back and drew herself a great curling moustache. 'I am a pirate,' she informed the cat. There was a ring at the front door bell. Lucy climbed back on the chair and drew frown lines and anger lines on her forehead and cheeks. 'I'm a terrible pirate,' she said.

The bell pealed louder and she went and lay down on the drawing-room floor and rolled herself tightly up in the sheepskin rug so that her head stuck out one end and her sandals the other. She closed her eyes. 'The Princess of Cleves is dead,' she said. There was a loud rap at the window and a voice called: 'LUCY — let me in this minute.'

Slowly Lucy unwound herself, unbolted the door and saw that a very small, plump lady with a felt hat and a short proud nose was standing in the wallflowers. Her hair was grey, her clothes were thick and tweedy and she was carrying an enormous brown paper bag. Nothing in the world could have looked less like the rose-petal girl in the photograph: yet Lucy knew at once, that moment, that here was Auntie Kitty.

'What in the world are you?' Auntie Kitty asked.

'I-I'm Lucy.'

'Are you alone?'

'Jake and Phyllis have gone for a walk. Father's at school and . . .'

'Yes?'

'Mother's . . .'

'Yes?'

'Mother's at the Fever House.'

'At the WHAT?'

'Phyllis says it's the Fever House.'

'It sounds dreadful!'

'It is.'

'Rubbish. Come with me.'

Auntie Kitty stepped carefully out of the wall-flowers and took Lucy's hand and they walked quietly through the garden and down the road to the bus-stop. Both Lucy's socks had gone to sleep in her sandals and she was wearing shorts with a tear in. She had only a thin blouse on and it was rather cold. The soot tickled.

'D'you think I ought to take my moustache off?' she asked.

'No,' said Auntie Kitty. She sat firmly down in the bus with the paper bag on her knee and in no time at all the bus reached the end of the dismal wooded road and they walked up the hill to the black door that said DO NOT OPEN THIS DOOR. 'What is the good of a door,' said Auntie Kitty, 'if you can't open it,' and they marched off round a corner of the laurel hedge, down a little path and came to a wicket leading to a kitchen garden.

'I am going to tell you three things,' said Auntie Kitty scanning the landscape, hand on the latch,

'Number One: This is a hospital where people go to be alone and not spread germs.

'Number Two: Children are not allowed to talk to the ill people even through the window. I think this is stupid, but it is a rule.

'Number Three: The ill people are not allowed to write letters because of germs on the paper. That is why your mother will not have written to you.'

Lucy felt suddenly, wonderfully happy. 'Will she get well?' she asked quite sensibly. 'Come and see,' said Auntie Kitty.

They went through the wicket and passed along the rows of peas. '*Good* afternoon,' said Auntie Kitty to a puzzled-looking gardener, '*good* afternoon,' to two very thin pale people in basket chairs and shawls, who looked quite frightened. They skirted a lavender hedge – and there was the Fever House. It was low and pretty and white with yellow roses growing all over it. Auntie Kitty paused to think, then they strode on, round a corner to a big, glassed-in veranda.

And there in a bed, looking pink and round and terribly bored sat Lucy's mother, gazing out at the garden.

Her mouth and her eyes flew wide open and her arms began to wave in all directions. She leaned over sideways, burrowed in a bag and, bouncing about on the bed, wrote on a piece of paper and held it up. It said 'Home on Monday.' She blew kisses, pulled faces and turned bright red.

Said Uncle

'There are people,' said Uncle,
'Who bumble like bees.
There are people,' said Uncle,
'With back to front knees.
There are people,' said Uncle,
'Who breathe through one ear.'
'There are people,' said Auntie,
'Who shouldn't drink beer.'

Richard Edwards

Aunt Louisa

When Aunt Louisa lit the gas
She had the queerest feeling.
Instead of leaving by the door
She vanished through the ceiling.

Max Fatchen

Life on Mars

Is there life on Mars? Yes, there is. I know because my Auntie Pat lived there for over three years. She went in October 1969 and worked as a garage pump attendant for a couple of months, before getting a good job in a shipping office. She reckoned it was much the same as anywhere else. During her stay she hitchhiked all over the planet, earning her keep as a waitress or chambermaid. She's got some really fantastic stories about Martians. Yes, there certainly is life on Mars. You ask my Auntie Pat.

Roger McGough

MARK TWAIN
FROM The Autobiography of Mark Twain

My Uncle, John A. Quarles, was also a farmer, and his place was in the country four miles from Florida. He had eight children and fifteen or twenty negroes and was also fortunate in other ways, particularly in his character I have not come across a better man than he was. I was his guest for two or three months every year, from the fourth year after we removed to Hannible till I was eleven or twelve years old . . . his farm has come very handy to me in literature once or twice. In *Huck Finn* and in *Tom Sawyer, Detective* I moved it down to Arkansas. It was all of six hundred miles but it was no trouble; it was not a very large farm – five hundred acres, perhaps but I could have done it if it had been twice as large . . .

It was a heavenly place for a boy, that farm of my uncle John's. The house was a double log one, with a spacious floor (roofed in) connecting it with the kitchen. In the summer the table was set in the middle of the shady and breezy floor, and the sumptuous meals – well, it makes me cry to think of them. Fried chicken, roast pig; wild and tame turkeys, duck and geese; venison just killed; squirrels, rabbits, pheasants, partridges, prairie-chickens; biscuits, hot batter cakes, hot buckwheat cakes, hot 'Wheat bread', hot rolls, hot corn pone; fresh corn boiled on the ear, succotash, butter-beans, string-beans, tomatoes, peas, Irish potatoes, sweet potatoes; buttermilk, sweet milk, 'clabber'; water-melons, muskmelons, cantaloupes – all fresh from the garden; apple pie, peach pie, pumpkin, apple dumplings, peach cobbler – I can't remember the rest.

My Uncle Paul of Pimlico

My Uncle Paul of Pimlico
Has seven cats as white as snow,
Who sit at his enormous feet
And watch him, as a special treat,
Play the piano upside-down,
In his delightful dressing gown;
The firelight leaps, the parlour glows,
And, while the music ebbs and flows,
They smile (while purring the refrains),
At little thoughts that cross their brains.

Mervyn Peake

Acknowledgements

The Publishers and the editor gratefully acknowledge permission to reprint copyright material to the following:

Faber and Faber Ltd for **My Sister Clarissa Spits Twice if I Kiss Her** from *To Aylsham Fair* by George Barker, and for excerpt from **The Children of Green Knowe** by Lucy M. Boston. Dell Books, a division of Bantam Doubleday Dell Publishing Group, Inc for excerpt from **The Night Swimmers** by Betsy Byars, copyright © 1980 by Betsy Byars. Charles Causley, Macmillan and David Higham Associates for **The Reverend Sabine Baring-Gould** from *Figgie Hobbin*, and **Family Album** from *Jack the Treacle Eater*, illustrated by Jill Bennett, copyright © Charles Causley, illustrated by Charles Keeping. The Penguin Group for **As Fit as a Fiddle** by Pauline Clarke from *Silver Bells and Cockle Shells* © Abelard Schumann. Morrow Junior Books, a division of William Morrow and Company, Inc for text of 'The Telephone Call' from **Ramona and her Mother** by Beverly Cleary, illustrated by Alan Tiegreen, text copyright © by Beverly Cleary, illustration copyright © 1979 by Alan Tiegreen. Faber & Faber for excerpt from **Absolute Zero** by Helen Cresswell, text copyright © Helen Cresswell, illustration copyright © Jill Bennett. George Allen & Unwin Ltd and Penguin Books Ltd for excerpt from **Charlie and the Chocolate Factory** by Roald Dahl, reprinted by permission of Murray Pollinger, Literary Agents, text copyright © Roald Dahl, accompanying illustration copyright © Michael Foreman. Penny Dann for illustration for **An Accident Happened to My Brother Jim** by Anon, illustration copyright © Penny Dann. HarperCollins Publishers Ltd for excerpt from **Birds, Beasts and Relatives** by Gerald Durrell. Richard Edwards for **Said Uncle**, copyright © Richard Edwards. Thomas Egan for **Dad's Friend, Jim**, copyright © Thomas Egan. Michael Joseph and David Higham Associates for **Mr Tom Narrow** and **The Quarrel** from *Silver Sand and Snow* by Eleanor Farjeon. Max Fatchen for **Aunt Louisa**, copyright © Max Fatchen. The Penguin Group for excerpt from **Goggle-Eyes** by Anne Fine, copyright © Anne Fine. Roy Fuller for **The National Union of Children** and **The National Association of Parents** from *Nine O'Clock Bell*, text copyright © Roy Fuller, illustration copyright © Jon Riley. Hamish Hamilton Ltd and Jane Gardam for exerpt from **Auntie Kitty and the Fever House**, copyright © Jane Gardam. The Executors of the Estate of Eve Garnett and Hutchinson and Co. for excerpt from **The Family From One End Street** by Eve Garnett. HarperCollins Publishers for excerpt from **Cheaper by the Dozen** by Frank B. Gilbreth, Jr. and Ernestine Gilbreth Carey, copyright © 1948, 1963 by Frank B. Gilbreth, Jr. and Ernestine Gilbreth Carey. Rumer Godden for excerpt from **A Time to Dance, No Time to Weep**, copyright © Rumer Godden. Reed Book Services and William Heinemann Ltd for excerpt from **Father and Son** by Edmund Gosse. The Penguin Group for excerpt from **The Children Who Lived in a Barn** by Eleanor Graham. Gregory Harrison for **Distracted the Mother Said to Her Boy**, text copyright © Gregory Harrison, published by Oxford University Press in *A Fourth Poetry Book 1982*, reprinted by permission of the author, illustration copyright © Jon Riley. Aitken & Stone for **Gloria, My Little Sister** © Russell Hoban. Mary Ann Hoberman for **Brother** from *The Book of Twentieth Century Children's Verse* (Viking), text copyright © Mary Ann Hoberman, illustration copyright © Michael Foreman. Shirley Hughes for illustration from **Little Women** by Louisa M. Alcott (Puffin Classics), illustration copyright © Shirley Hughes. Tove Jansson for excerpts from